I0689039

AFFLICTION INCLUDED

AFFLICTION INCLUDED

STEVEN T. BRAMBLE

LONG BEACH   OAKLAND

For Elaine Tolle Simpson

ZQ-287

ZQ-287 Press
3942 E. 4th St.
Long Beach, CA, 90814
www.zq287.com

ISBN 978-1-7325766-0-5

BY STEVEN T. BRAMBLE

Grid City Overload

Disposable Thought

PREMORBID

1

Two days before a business trip to India I unexpectedly found myself hospitalized with a severe case of food poisoning. I had been preparing for the trip for over a month, educating myself on the particularities of intellectual property rights and patenting in the Southeastern Zone. The purpose of the trip was to sell a major Indian conglomerate the rights to use a chemical Basil & Crittenden had developed for a hair gel product that was generating huge profits. My role as Head of Cultural Marketing Relations for B&C was geared toward that kind of byzantine task: administering transactions between corporate entities located in different zones and internations, making my benign-sounding title somewhat misleading. There was of course not a lot of official reason to need an emissary with any sort of expertise in navigating cultural differences, but multinationals still had to deal with the reality that world culture remained some ways off from being fully homogenized, despite the eager positivity of World Organization messaging. Which isn't to say world culture was a total pack of lies, either. The majority of important cultural variations had already melted away, but still there remained a noticeable veneer of regional—even national—distinctions, no matter how uncomfortable the fact. For that reason, people like myself were still necessary to the process.

I had been adrift on a half-hour lunch break somewhere in the middle of a vast 75-hour workweek, consuming the contents of a small microwaveable bowl of meat chili bought from one of the vendors on the B&C campus, when I encountered something in the food that didn't taste quite right but that I ate anyway. Only an hour later my bone marrow seemed to have become rotten, skin so sensitive the smallest touch caused pain, and stomach full of projectile ammunition. Traces of blood in my vomit drove me to check in at New Boston Central.

I called my section supervisor from my hospital bed.

"This one was important, Stanly," Andrea said through the phone. "The Board was counting on you being available."

"I understand," I said, barely able to speak without throwing up.

"We're unable to reschedule, so we'll have to send your assistant in your place."

"All right. My apologies to the Board."

"I probably don't have to tell you this kind of sickness likely won't be tolerated a second time."

"Of course."

"As of now they're reassigning you on a trip to Ghana in four days to meet with Abeeku Boateng, the CEO of Kente, Inc., about a proposal to acquire Flourisaide toothpaste. This is all pending the results of your psych eval, so make sure you submit your clearance as soon as possible. We'll send along your itinerary and all the necessary documentation."

I spent several days laying in New Boston Central at the center of an intricate web of tubes, wires and beeping instruments like a creature caught, immobilized. I was lucky not to have been fired for missing the trip given my liability to the company. Very rarely was I extended any leniency, and most often I found myself being blatantly ostracized. What kept my employment alive at Basil &

Crittenden was my reliability, along with the surprising fact, for both my immediate superiors and the Board, that I was not the kind of person my past suggested I was. I was a rarity in the corporate professional world, someone with limited political rights and a poor mental health classification who had managed to achieve a respectable position. If I didn't recover in four days' time, however, that position would be jeopardized.

By the third day the doctor told me I still wasn't fully convalesced (not to mention I was apparently one of the worst food poisoning cases she'd seen in recent memory), but finally she agreed after I pleaded with her gratuitously to sign a B&C form stating I was well enough to return to work. Before being discharged from the hospital I had to undergo a mandatory psych eval. This was true for all outgoing patients of any hospital worldwide, but because of my family history all psych evals were potentially dangerous, and I was routinely subjected to overly rigorous questioning.

A nurse alerted me to the arrival of my evaluator, who turned out to be a tightly-wound guy in his early 30s with a bureaucratic haircut and thin lips he bit on all throughout the process of setting up his recording equipment. He didn't bother with a greeting when he entered the room, or even eye contact with me, and went about the procedures of getting his materials ready in total silence. He was going to be a very tough evaluator. Physically he was somewhat small, poorly dressed, and his morning shave had irritated his skin, but I could feel my heartbeat drumming in terror of him, watching from the hospital bed in my weakened state a set of humorless, efficient eyes working behind his glasses. He sat down in a chair across from my bed with a groan, situated himself, pressed a button to begin recording, skimmed briefly through my file on his tablet.

"This is Evlt. Roorback conducting psych eval on one Stanly Borque," he announced for the sake of the recording, proceeding to slur through the date, time, evaluator number, etc., in pure monotone boredom. "I'm required by law to inform you that this evaluation will be made available to both the W.O. government and also to private employers. You have the right to claim exemption from this evaluation according to WL 2-38(i). Should you claim exemption, you will be required to appear in court to contest the mandate. You have the right to a public attorney. Do you understand these statements?"

"Yes."

"Okay then, Mr. Borque," he said, transitioning to a more condescending tone, "you obviously know the drill here, but for my benefit let's get some basic information out of the way. I see here you've been diagnosed with a disorder?"

His eyes flicked up at me from his screen.

"Yes, borderline personality," I said.

"Mm-hm. And I also see here you're a felon? Would you mind stating what your felony is for the record, please?"

I swallowed. Prompting me to make statements like this about myself was unusual in comparison to all other times I'd been evaluated.

"Lower treason. But I'm sure you can see the situation was a bit complicated."

"Yes?" he said, placing two fingers over his chin.

I closed my eyes, unable to help my own fury at what seemed like pointless provocation. "The charge was applied to me because of my mother's political activity and what the court perceived as my connection to it, not necessarily because of my own actions. So there was an important degree of nuance to the ruling."

The nuance being they wanted to classify me as a social pariah in order to purge the son of a treasonous political dissident from mainstream society.

"Your father was also charged with lower treason."

"Along the same legal lines, yes." I rolled my head on the pillow to look at the ceiling.

"So what we have here is someone not only classified as borderline personality, but also convicted of a felony, as you yourself have just explained to me." Although he was small his voice intoned with the iron of sadistic officialdom. "And yet"—he adjusted his glasses and leaned forward—"here you are as head of an overseas marketing department for no less than Basil & Crittenden. Seems to me you've gone through quite the reinvention."

This aggressiveness, on the other hand, was completely typical of most evaluators I'd encountered in the past, though I had never encountered one as immediately belligerent as him. In a way it calmed me down, his standard reaction of resentment and disgust at my file. I said nothing in response, only held his gaze with the most neutral expression possible.

"How is it you've managed to find yourself in this occupation, Mr. Borque?"

I hesitated, an enormous wheel of hot, emotional responses spinning through my head before I steadied myself and answered in the least amount of words possible. "I'm not my mother."

"And what exactly do you mean by that?"

"What I mean is—" I cleared my throat and put a hand on my stomach. "What I mean is that my mother's beliefs are not my own." My stress level had built up so fast I had almost forgotten how nauseated I was before he came into the room. Something in my stomach felt like it was being tugged tight, and I reached desperately down for a small grey bucket on the floor. "The truth is I never actually agreed with her on much of—"

In the middle of my sentence I heaved once and then expelled watery brown vomit into the bucket. I was forced to sit there, face flushed red, and spit the remainder of my shame away in front of the evaluator, who was impatiently scrutinizing a bit of dirt under one of his fingernails.

"Would you like me to call a nurse in?" he asked with detached professionalism. "Obviously I'm unable to attend to you."

I inhaled deeply, burbled out, "No, it's okay. I feel better now." I couldn't afford to let him leave and possibly delay my psych eval clearance since I had to be on a plane to Ghana the next morning. I couldn't help but notice with a small note of satisfaction that my regurgitation had ceased to show any signs of blood.

I quickly put the bucket on the floor to the opposite side of the bed. "I'm okay, let's continue."

He contemplated my physical state for a moment before gesturing me to complete my explanation.

"I never aided my mother in any of her political activity," I reaffirmed, now propping myself into a sitting position.

"Neither did you make any attempts to stop her."

I said in a tone I hoped was cleansed of any sarcasm whatsoever, "I was young. And unfortunately she happened to be my mother."

He nodded vacantly at my file, which he was back to perusing with predatory smugness. He looked through the top half of his glasses. "Still unmarried?"

"Yes."

"Trouble making connections with people, or just disinterested?"

"I'm usually traveling abroad. That makes it difficult. And given my past, I prefer to focus on my work."

"I see you're on Pentafalex. Have you been sticking to your dosage?"

"Yes, sir."

"Any thoughts of self-harm lately, Mr. Borque?"

"No."

"Not at all? Depression, listlessness, nothing like that?"

"No. As a matter of fact, I've been productive. I was supposed to be on a business trip right now conducting an intellectual property rights transfer, but they've had to adjust my schedule to accommodate my recovery. I'm trying to get well so I can go back to work tomorrow."

This was a tactic I had found effective against evaluators in the past. Listing out some details relevant to my job reminded them I had ascended to quite a high station in spite of my damning personal history, one much higher than they themselves held, and it tended to elicit respect, even if the respect was only begrudging or resentful.

Rather than putting Roorback on his heels, he merely side-stepped my maneuver and jabbed me in yet another vulnerable spot. "Your father committed suicide when you were at the age of twenty-one, is that correct?"

My face now flushed red for a different reason. There was something bizarre about the way he was going about this, something needlessly derogatory in it that I had never experienced before, like the way he stated my exact age at the time of my father's suicide. The detail was shocking, especially to hear it delivered in his imperious tone. A feeling of helplessness washed through me.

He jabbed even harder. "A gunshot wound to the head, correct?"

I heard grains of anger beginning to filter into my voice. "Correct. But a lot of people my age had a parent kill themselves when they were young."

"Well, not everyone," he said, seeming to imply he was exempt from the statement.

Something wasn't right. I wondered if he had something against me personally to insult me like this, or if I had done something wrong I was unaware of. Even if most evaluators abused their authority when confronted with my case, always making sure to harass me and keep me in a marginalized state of mind, it never reached a point of outright invective, not even after my father killed himself and I was designated borderline personality as a continuing punitive measure against my mother's treason. The way Roorback was questioning me seemed like he was trying to make me mad on purpose. I sank into abject fear, realizing the arbitrary whims of this evaluator could get me terminated from B&C and locked away in a psych facility. There was nothing I could do except answer his questions and hope for it to be over.

"And what about your mother? Is she still alive?"

"Yes," I said, in the process of disassociating myself from the situation in order to guard against any emotional response. "But she's been in maximum security prison for years and I've fallen out of touch with her."

"Tell me, Mr. Borque, what were the reasons for your father's suicide?"

This was all unnecessary. He didn't have to ask me any of this. It was all right in front of him—it was all in my file.

My father took a shower the day he killed himself. By the time he was lying dead, the towel he used to dry himself off must have still been damp. I don't know why my mind constantly latches onto that detail, his still-damp towel. Far more often than makes sense to me I envision him washing his hair that morning, as if his appearance was still going to matter to him throughout the rest of the day, which for him lasted only another hour or so.

He did it on a Sunday, in the one-bedroom apartment we had begun renting after losing our old two-story house in New Boston. This was when I was 21, almost five years after my mother had been sent to prison on charges of treason and all the trouble surrounding that event had mostly quieted down for us.

I had been studying for a financial accounting test. Even though my felony and borderline personality classification practically guaranteed I would never get a high-paying job, I had gone ahead and enrolled in an accelerated five-year master of business course at New Boston Polytechnic. My father had been pessimistic about the idea—not without reason, given what he had gone through after his own lower treason charge and clinical depression classification. (Our status changes in mental health had clearly been orchestrated. Aside from the fact we had both been undergoing regular psych evals for years with no such adverse results, both of our new diagnoses were delivered almost simultaneously, only one month after the completion of our joint trial.) Our attorney had advised us it would be futile to contest the charges because the lower treason felony was largely symbolic, used in cases of political repression. The good news was it would carry no prison time so long as we pled guilty. Still, the sentencing meant my father would be immediately terminated from his directorship with Logan-Barr Mass Transit, and would be disqualified from holding any occupation other than low-wage service or manual labor jobs. At the time of his death he was working as a dishwasher for a restaurant located on the Strider Solutions corporate campus in Prospectville. After sinking so low, he couldn't help but discourage me from placing my own hopes in a career, urging me to go into a trade instead. Young and blissfully ignorant as I was, I decided not to listen to him.

You hear so many people who had second breakdown generation parents tell their stories that you can forget your own, incredible as that sounds. But sometimes I can remember so clearly.

I didn't look up from my book when he emerged from his room, poured himself a bowl of cereal, and sat down at the table. I was memorizing double-entry accounting. He worked night shifts at the restaurant, so he was usually groggy and not very talkative in the mornings. I remember blocking out the sound of his spoon clinking against the bowl, the crunching sounds of his eating. I was zeroed in on the book, frantically scribbling notes. I heard him set the bowl aside, sitting in silence before he uttered my name.

"Stanly."

I laid down my pen.

He was slumped in his chair, bleary and practically hungover with exhaustion. His hair was combed, still wet with product after his shower, which he always took first thing in the morning. My father's face normally had the kind of temperate expression you tend to see with educated people, but that morning his countenance had collapsed, and he seemed to be wavering on the point of something almost like anger. His cereal sat on the table, unfinished.

"Stanly," he repeated.

"*Yes*," I said, more than a little irritated at having had my concentration broken.

"I don't think I can do it today."

"Do what?"

His vision remained riveted down at the table. "Go to work again."

This was a common refrain from him. He hated working his dishwashing job. Most of the time I felt I could understand. I had a warehouse job that wasn't exactly a joy. The difference, of course, was that his job was a humiliation, a degradation of his former life that had mutilated him and left him permanently disfigured. Many times I had tried to help him to reconcile with his new fate, but it was always evident, even when he made the effort to cheer up and accept the way things were, that he could not make peace with the disaster which had laid waste to him and to our family. This time was different, though. His complaint rang out like a child's, maudlin and helpless, and for some reason that only added to my aggravation.

"I don't know what to tell you, dad," I answered sharply. "If you can't find another job, you're going to have to learn how to deal with this one."

He didn't respond, didn't react, only kept his vision trained at the table, finally saying, "I don't think your mother ever loved me."

"What? What are you talking about?"

"She never wanted to listen to me. I told her what all this would bring down on us if she didn't stop, but she never cared. And now look."

I picked up my pen and tapped it against the pages of my book. "You're over-thinking. You need to calm down."

My mother was what most people would call an ultra-nationalist. She was arrested for being a member of a small conspiratorial anti-W.O. group which she helped to found called Identity For All. The IFA had the laughable goal of establishing an international network of resistance aimed at overthrowing the World Organization of Zone Coalition Governments and Internations. How she intended to accomplish all that was never very clear to me, but it did earn her a life sentence in prison, along with politically repressive felonies for my father and I, something I had worked hard to come to terms with over the years, and my father's stagnancy in his own puddle of misery slowly had become a burden.

He shook his head in defiance of my scolding. "I agreed with her beliefs, Stanly. You know that. I supported her in her activism, went to her speaking engagements, and never once did I tell her to stop. Only to be careful. But even that she ignored."

"Dad, what's this about? I'm trying to study."

"I just can't see how someone who loved us would do this."

"You have to stop thinking about her so much. How many times have I said that?"

"Things are just so ruined," he said, voice gnarled with pain.

At the time I thought he was being dramatic, but remembering all this now I have to admit it's hard to picture my father as he was before, a successful civil engineer who provided for our family, who was happy in his work and home life. My mother, by comparison, was a natural-born crusader, constantly aggravated or incensed by one thing or another, and sanctimonious of almost everyone who didn't share her opinions. Sometimes that sanctimony had extended towards my father, the man who previously existed—the good husband, the kind father, the hard worker— and also the man who had mostly vanished from my memory. Whenever I did think about him after his death, all I was able to summon to my mind was his hollowed-out shell, terrified of his dishwashing job, sitting across from me at the breakfast table.

"It's going to get better."

"No," he asserted, looking up from the table.

He almost never raised his voice to me.

"Things," he said, fighting to verbalize his thoughts but still speaking forcefully, "things really are different now. There's no way to change anything, we can't control what happens to us. We get to go on living, but for what?"

"Dad, it's—"

"And if you can't make your own destiny, can't hope for anything, then what are you? That means you're a piece of errata, no will, no effect or influence. That means you don't exist. You're just inert, like some kind of device. Some kind of recording device."

I struggled to process what he meant, searching for some way to counter his depression. "What would mom say to that, that you have no effect or influence? She would be horrified."

"Stanly, you're mother is going to be in prison for the rest of her life. She only *imagined* she could change things. Her beliefs were admirable, but that doesn't mean they were correct."

"Dad, what can I say that's going to change anything? I think maybe you should get some more sleep before work today, you seem tired and too much inside your own head. I can't really understand you."

He dropped his gaze against the table again. I watched him sit in silence, thinking to myself, *is this really happening?* In a way it was like his clinical depression classification had become a self-fulfilling prophecy. Of course you always hear peoples' stories about the suicide of a parent or grandparent—nearly everybody has one. My mother had told me once or twice about my own grandfather committing suicide during the breakdown generation and how bizarre, how frightening it was to see such a mass of people on a global scale taking their own lives. There's the constant anti-suicide public messaging and the mandatory psych evals, which my mother believed the World Org used to exploit peoples' fears and exert control over the population, one conviction of hers she was far from alone in having. But no matter how much you hear about it, or how much you think you know, nothing prepares you for when it happens. There's something unbelievable about it, a creepy surreality of death taking hold of a person from within, dragging them down not with the force of sickness or injury, but with the force of logic, hopelessness. I knew something was wrong with my father in that moment, but I was unable to do anything. What *could* I have done? I justify myself, looking back, that my silence was possibly an act of respecting his wishes.

"Maybe you're right," he said. "I think I'm going to go back to sleep."

He picked up his cereal bowl, took it to the sink and washed it, walked back to his room, not strangely or in any way that would've hinted at what he was about to do, but still his movements were threaded with a taut, reverberating anxiousness.

I looked out the window down onto the view of the parking lot, glancing back at the book and my notes, considering going back to studying, but I didn't. I see so much of myself in my failure to do anything that day, in the implicit passivity that my mother was always trying to train out of me.

Considering how much her actions and beliefs played a role in shaping the course of my life, my mother's character and concerns never much transferred on to me. She took great care to educate me from an early age about what she viewed as the crimes and aberrant ideology of the World Organization. Her political stance, which I got to know ad nauseam over the course of my childhood—that individual nation-state sovereignty should be revived, democracy instituted, and the legal right to identity pluralism declared—was somewhat ironic given that she started her political career as a government employee of the North American Zone writing up anthropo-sociological white papers for internal use in the world culture initiative. She'd been tapped from her professorship by the W.O. to aid in furthering the drive toward worldwide assimilation of markets by eliminating almost all distinctions between peoples, especially national and regional differences. During my parents' generation world culture was only just starting to take hold, and there was still an open debate, though gradually narrowing, about its morality and implications for the future. She quit her job at the Department of World Culture after three years and became a lifelong militant critic of the very program she had helped along. For the better part of the decade that followed she was essentially a professional political activist, all of it culminating in her IFA activities and arrest. My relationship with her got more contentious the older I got because, although I thought her basic interpretation of how the world worked was for the most part correct, and even that she had some good points about the moral pitfalls of world culture and W.O. policy, I could never be persuaded by her that the World Org was inherently evil. The truth was I didn't think much about politics. She saw the World Org as a bid for the global supremacy of "Western" ideology, an outdated term she used often that I confess I never got the hang of, and the Organization's core principle of reversing environmental deterioration as a pretense for consolidating what she termed "total oligarchy." I always felt like somewhat of an idiot around her, and in my worst moments like a disappointment. Where I was concerned about my own happiness, following a successful path, and girls, she was concerned about enormous interlocking theories, current events, and principles of humanity. I even found her political monomania heroic at times, but I couldn't get myself to follow her example. More agreeable to me was my father's career, which provided for our family and seemed to afford him at least a modicum of pleasure. I saw myself in that.

From the bedroom came the enormous bark of a pistol shot. I flinched in my chair and made the slightest, sharpest inhalation of breath. I made no sound. Did not move. For quite a while afterwards.

Evlt. Roorback finished typing notes into my file. Before giving his diagnosis, he retrieved a small bottle from his bag and dispensed some medicated lotion that he used on his face and neck, his skin apparently irritated by something more serious than just his morning shave.

"Mr. Borque, are you familiar with the word 'premorbidity'?"

"Pre...?"

"*Morbidity*. The word can be used to describe a patient's mental state before the onset of a disease, or a change in cognitive functioning. However, for individuals such as yourself, who suffer from serious conditions that can flare up, or simply become progressively worse over time, we can sometimes define these individuals as entering a premorbid phase."

"What does that mean?" I asked. I had never heard this before, and it seemed like there was the possibility he wasn't going to clear my file.

He coughed into his shirt sleeve several times. "You've exhibited several prodromes over the course of this evaluation which indicate—"

"Excuse me, sorry, what was the word? Prodromes?"

"Yes, prodromes. *Symptoms*, Mr. Borque. Symptoms which indicate to me you've moved into a premorbid phase. Or, in different terms, that you're exhibiting qualities in your evaluation responses that are leading me to the conclusion your borderline personality disorder is worsening."

I sat propped up in the bed, completely stunned. Given the fact I didn't have borderline personality disorder in the first place, that I had only been stuck with the classification as a form of political punishment, the only thing I could think was maybe Roorback was looking for some justification to exploit my situation for his own benefit.

"Not to overstep my bounds, sir, but are you positive? I've never heard this before. My last eval was only a few months ago, and I wasn't told anything out of the ordinary by the evaluator."

"I'm quite positive. Sometimes a condition can advance rapidly, or even all at once. Usually without the patient noticing anything is wrong."

"And what happens if I move beyond a premorbid phase?"

Again he started coughing, harder this time, as if he were becoming sick right in front of me. "Should you move into a morbid phase from a premorbid, you would require treatment at a psych facility."

My stomach churned at his words. I tried to speak but was unable, and to my own horror I leaned over the side of my bed where I had placed the grey bucket and released an acrid-tasting cord of vomit. I could feel my heartbeat tapping furiously against the arm I had rolled over on. I turned back to Roorback slowly, fearful of how he would interpret what had just happened. The food poisoning hadn't helped, but the last thing I had expected to hear at the start of the evaluation was that I might soon be sent to a psych facility.

To my amazement, he actually seemed to take pity on me, even if that pity did come in the form of a laugh and a tenor of superiority in his reassurance. "Try not to worry, Mr. Borque. Sending you to a psych facility is not my goal here. I'm going to increase your dosage of Pentafalex, which should work to reduce these symptoms."

I couldn't believe it. He had the nerve to tell me not to worry right after informing me there was a likelihood I could be sent to a psych facility gulag for a mental disorder I didn't even have? And why the change in tone? Through the entire evaluation he had been screwing with my head, forcing me to answer unnecessary questions about the most painful moments of my life, and now he was on *my* side?

"Sir," I said, hearing my own desperation, "I don't mean to be rude, but would you be able to tell me what it was about my responses that led you to this conclusion?"

Yet again he broke into a coughing fit, and this time it was especially bad. I could hear the sound coming from deep in his lungs, his face becoming branched with veins, ballooning a hypertensive pink color. "Excuse me, excuse me," he said through his hacking.

"Please," I said. "It would put my mind at ease to know."

Through the tail-end of his convulsions and with a hand flung against his chest he managed to get out, "Yes, yes, I understand, but unfortunately I'm unable to help you in that matter. These prodromes happen to be quite technical, and—"

"Is there a legal reason why I shouldn't know?"

"—and it would be difficult to translate them into layman's terms, and, yes, um, I would have to check on the precise legality of such a disclosure, but I can certainly look into it and let you know."

What a pathetic pair we were in that hospital room. One man who couldn't stop puking and another who couldn't stop coughing. He had put a terrible fear into me. "I see, well I would very much appreciate any information you can provide. But I have to ask, will this premorbid phase interfere with me returning to work tomorrow?"

His coughing continued, and it was beginning to grate on me. "Oh, I don't think it'll be an issue." He got up from the chair to stop the recording and began packing up his equipment at a haphazard pace, as if he'd just then realized he was late for something important. "I'll send along the work clearance, as well as the prescription for your new dosage. If there won't be anything else, Mr. Borque, you'll have to excuse me, I have another evaluation I need to get to."

"Of course," I said, unable to believe he had put me through all that just to summarily give me clearance and up the dosage of my medication.

Without another word he turned and rushed out, coughing the entire way.

With not a little physical suffering, I made it onto my flight to Ghana the next day. Still, I was surprised at my own resilience. I had expected to feel worse. The only thing to do to keep my mind off it was to study the proposal sent to B&C from Abeeku Boateng to acquire Fluorisaide. I was surprised to learn that apparently Boateng had been requesting a meeting with a representative from Basil & Crittenden for quite some time.

Andrea had briefed me over the phone during the flight. "We can't be sure, but this might be about more than Fluorisaide."

"Any idea what it is he wants from us?" I asked.

"Not really, but whatever it is, the Board has expressed disinterest. He has a reputation for being somewhat megalomaniacal, as well as for having more nationalist sympathies than someone in his position ought to, which is why we're sending you. Make sure you keep this as diplomatic as possible. You've been given the authority to green-light the Fluorisaide deal, but anything beyond that and we want you to deflect it with as much tact as possible."

I hadn't understood why they were sending someone of my limited stature with no support staff, or even a legal adviser, to speak with the most powerful CEO in the African Zone, but now I was starting to put the pieces together. If Boateng had ambitious plans for some kind of deal with B&C, the feeling apparently wasn't mutual, and they needed an ambassador to maintain relations. Fluorisaide was simply being granted as a pre-approved olive branch.

Within the company I was considered an internations expert.

The territorial lines of the former countries of the world, despite what W.O. dogma constantly claimed, had not been reduced merely to areas of regional administration. Internations still represented an identity to their inhabitants, despite enormous efforts by the Department of World Culture to remold peoples' provincialisms into a single, seamless conception of a unified population spanning the globe. Much of my expertise on internations came from the education my mother had forced upon me about the diversity of world cultures. Ironically, that same subversive curriculum became the reason why Basil & Crittenden tapped me for their cultural marketing division. Even though publicly they had to maintain the official stance that cultural distinctions within the world market didn't exist, most corporations found themselves in the tricky situation of having to cultivate whole departments of specialists who could facilitate business between foreign entities. Developing talent in-house for such purposes had become almost impossible in the political climate of world culture, which made someone like me a valuable asset—even with my controversial background. So if Boateng was indeed a right-wing nationalist, then I was the natural choice.

My weakened state notwithstanding, I finally started to loosen up during the long flight to Ghana. I had managed to avoid missing any more work, and other than the strange episode of the psych eval with Roorback things were back to normal. All I had to do was sit in first-class and relax. Most of the way there I slept, keeping the sound of movies and TV piped into my headphones so as not to have to listen to my own thoughts.

During my three-hour layover in Brasília I caught up on the news and read the overview of Kente, Inc. I had been provided. The corporation was a behemoth, accountable for just over twenty percent of the African Zone's total GDP, mostly due to the fact that Ghana had fewer environmental problems than most other internations on the continent. For that reason Kente's government mandate had been made quite a bit larger than those of the other multinationals in the zone.

Boateng himself was an interesting case. He hadn't been connected in any way to the previous CEO, Viktor Moyoyo, whose father had been installed into the corporation just after the consolidation of the World Org. Apparently Boateng had started out for Kente as a financial analyst, and somewhere along the way Moyoyo had decided to take him under his wing. Under Boateng's leadership the corporation had expanded aggressively. His personality profile painted a fairly bold picture.

A. Boateng is enterprising personality, complete with classic traits of type. Stands out in position because unique career path, begun outside traditional elite circles. Known for highly manipulative intelligence, committed right-wing worldview, magnified self-importance. Rapport with lower classes strong.

Even if I was going to be sticking to a very limited script during this meeting, it still seemed reckless for Andrea not to have coached me at least a little on how to deal with this man. It was possible she had been preoccupied with the India deal and had looked at this whole assignment as an afterthought. Either way it was different from the way things normally operated.

By the time I woke up in New Accra an entire day had passed since my departure and I was sad to leave the solitude and comfort of the flight behind. I felt I could sleep endlessly, and probably would have if allowed to.

We disembarked onto the runway in a hot, muggy rain. The early morning sky was a greenish-grey, and the air smelled potent, equatorial. Toward the bottom of the long L-shaped ramp I saw a retinue of dark-suited men standing beneath black umbrellas. Boateng was not difficult to spot amongst them. He was wearing a handsome cream-colored Panama suit and hat and was a full head taller than the rest of his guards. I felt a bit uneasy that he deemed it worth his time to come meet me at the airport personally, but if he was upset at the fact that I had arrived alone he didn't show it. He was smiling ear-to-ear as I approached him.

"Welcome to Ghana, Mr. Borque," he said over the sound of the rain and jet engines. He held out his hand and gave a pleasant handshake. "I am very excited you are here."

"Thank you, Mr. Boateng. I appreciate the pick-up." My suit coat was already soaked.

"Of course, of course. Follow me this way, please. We have a car waiting." His English was unabashedly accented for a CEO. Already a sign of his nationalist tendencies.

We began walking in the direction of two silver SUVs parked about 40 meters away, flanked closely by the dark-suited men. The rain hitting the ceiling of umbrellas above created a kind of acoustic bubble that moved with us across the runway. One of the men broke off and opened the door of the lead car for Boateng and I. We stepped into the backseat and the door was shut behind us, the rest of the men filing into the other vehicle.

"That is much better," Boateng said, removing his hat and getting comfortable. He had a close-cropped haircut with two illustrious streaks of white at his temples. On his side of the car there was a small combination refrigerator and humidor built into the door panel. "Tell me, is this your first time in Ghana?"

I ran my fingers through my own hair, which had also been soaked. "Yes, actually. It's my first time visiting the African Zone."

"Ghana is a very beautiful place," he said, putting his fingers together out in front of him to punctuate the statement. "I have been all over the world, and no place is as beautiful to me. In fact, I would like to take you on a short drive to show you my city. It has always been my opinion that New Accra is most beautiful in the rain." His expression was good-natured, energetic. He seemed genuinely excited to show me around.

"I would like that very much."

"Excellent. I hope you are not too tired from your journey?"

"Just the opposite," I had to admit. I was feeling better than I had since coming down with food poisoning almost a week ago. "I had a restful flight."

"Very well, then. We will tour the city and then get you settled at the hotel."

The car started and we were off.

"Do you smoke, Mr. Borque?" He reached into the humidor

and extracted a coffee-brown cigar with a black and gold band.

"Thank you, no. I'm still getting over a nasty case of food poisoning."

"*Bea-yah*, I am sorry to hear that. Will it bother you too much if I smoke?"

"Please, go right ahead."

"Thank you. My wife tells me all the time that I have a greater love for cigars than for her." He cracked the window just enough to ventilate the smoke, sounds of the rain and road cutting into the backseat like a thin blade. While he was preparing the cigar, he said, "I suspect you have heard the stories about me being a right-wing demon, eh?"

I laughed. "One or two, yes."

"People cannot understand the pride I have for my home, my people. The same pride as I have for these things, I have for my business."

I wasn't sure how to respond. Even just to say *my people* during a psych eval, for a normal person, with all its implications of national identity, would be a dangerous move. I didn't doubt he had looked into my file before I arrived and seen my own background concerning charges of nationalism. Maybe for this reason he felt comfortable speaking his mind, but it had the effect of setting me on edge.

The car trundled through a series of gates before inching its way into the airport's orbit of dense traffic.

"Do you always travel in such a large group?" I asked, referring to the car full of dark-suited men traveling behind us. There had been ten of them, all armed.

"Yes," he said, falling into a graver attitude than before. "Unfortunately, security has become more of a concern lately." He struck a match and went about the process of lighting the cigar, which had a sweet, almost fruit-like smell. "But you have no reason to worry. Have you read my proposal to acquire Fluorisaide?"

"I have. But I meant to ask you"—I reached into my pocket for my mobile to pull up the document—"I noticed while I was going over it that there was no initial bid listed. I'm sure it was just a mistake, but I wanted to check with you to make sure I didn't overlook—"

"I am sure you did not miss anything important, but, please, Mr. Borque, look."

We had made it away from the airport, the car now humming down a freeway, tropical greenery spilling at the road's edges. Through Boateng's window the skyline of New Accra was visible, half-shrouded in the grey robes of the downpour, the tallest buildings standing against the sky in the ascetic slate-blue color of world culture architecture, pragmatically geometrical and without exaggeration.

"It's striking," I said.

His tone was unsatisfied. "In a certain way, yes, you are right. It is very modern."

The drive into the city wasn't long, and soon we were in the heart of downtown. The streets were wide boulevards flanked by the towering economic and corporate buildings we had seen only minutes before from the freeway. The look of everything was hardly different at all from the downtown area where my offices were located in New Boston, the same slate-blue or marble-white architecture, many of the entrances to the buildings preceded by semi-circular plazas with fountains or abstract sculptures. Boateng sat smoking his cigar in a kind of trance, watching out the window without speaking much. I took the hint and concentrated on the city passing by in my own window.

"This, of course, is the financial district. The main W.O. buildings can also be found here."

There were very few people on the street because of the rain, but the ones who were out wore suits or general office clothing. The boulevards swarmed with black business sedans and shiny red taxis. Gradually we passed out of the core of the downtown area, and replacing the skyscrapers were stores, restaurants, bars, and upscale apartment buildings, all still in the style of world culture architecture. Again, this was a familiar scene from New Boston, an almost identical copy of the neighborhood where I lived. I recognized the names of many of the businesses. These were the people who worked in the towers, for either a corporate employer or the World Org. Boateng remained silent, fixated on his window. I kept stealing glances at him to gauge how I should possibly be reacting to all this but he was unreadable, smoke gliding around his head like a mane. Watching him smoking an expensive cigar and taking in the sights of his de facto empire through the window tint became surreal to me, almost a bit frightening. His intensity had completely usurped his earlier friendliness, and I began to wonder what the point of this was.

Suddenly his face came to life. "Ah, here we are."

I looked out my window and saw we were now in a poorer neighborhood. The houses and apartments were different from anything I'd ever seen before. They still showed signs of world culture architecture, but rather than being purely one thing they were a patchwork, frankenstein facades put together with varying types of materials. There was more color, more expression, and not just in the buildings. The streets were crowded with people. A great deal of them wore thin tunics, intricately and garishly patterned in every hue. Their umbrellas, too, were a flowing river of vivid discs. Things seemed more alive, more fluid.

Boateng became so excited he almost shouted. "Ah ha! This is what I intend to show you here, look." He pointed out my window at a large polyurethane canopy set up at the edge of an intersection. Underneath it was a small makeshift kitchen fuming inviting-looking steam from enormous kettles, women with long yellow dresses and thick dreadlocks laboring over them, preparing food with bare hands. There was also a small dining area composed of plastic tables and chairs where people were eating, sheltered from the rain. "Do you know what this is, Mr. Borque?"

"No," I said. I had never seen anything like it.

"Here in Ghana we call this a chop bar."

"Chop bar?"

"Yes. It is an open-air restaurant on the street. And look down here."

We stopped at another intersection where there was a large volume of foot traffic. Taking up the entirety of the street in both directions was a labyrinth of the same kinds of polyurethane canopies, a twisting, unending chain of people with bags in their hands moving through them.

"This is the Dansoman market. I have brought you here because this is where my favorite chop bar is. I have not breakfasted yet. Please, come join me."

I was a bit stunned when he opened the door and stepped out into the rain amongst the droves of people, and I hesitated a moment before getting out of the car. Even though I had heard the term "market" many times during my extracurricular studies with my mother, I had never actually seen one. The seeming complexity of it, the huge numbers of people, intimidated me. Not to mention there would undoubtedly be pictures of this event that would surface later, making me easy prey for any psych evaluator with the mind to bag themselves an accused nationalist. Not that I had any choice. I got out into the rain, which had withered away to a drizzle, and found two of Boateng's guards already approaching me with hoisted umbrellas. There was a lot of noise, the sounds of people yelling and laughing, a living commotion I had never experienced before. As I feared, I was utterly conspicuous. The people who passed by gawked at me, and I felt out of place. Boateng, on the other hand, coming around the car with his own pair of guards to meet me, was beaming with joy again, smiling at me as he had at the airport. His hat was back on and he was still smoking the cigar. The people stared at him, too, but he was not the least bit uncomfortable. He put a hand on my shoulder and extended his arm agreeably.

"Come, follow me."

We started off with our silent, dark-suited escorts against the currents of people, the eyes of all the people entering our vicinity attaching themselves to us. Women, running children, old men with silver hair and glasses, small laughing groups of teenagers, young couples holding hands, all staring. I felt embarrassed, even a little obscene, like we were making a spectacle of ourselves with our armed guards and expensive clothing here in this more modest and unassuming setting. Some of that feeling dissipated when Boateng began waving at almost every shop owner we passed, calling out to them in words I couldn't understand. We came to a large canopy with a dining area full of people and a handwritten sign standing in front. OUR GHANA'S EVERLASTING GLORY CHOP BAR.

"Here we are, the best chop bar in all of Dansoman." He said this with his cigar stuck between exuberant teeth.

A short woman with a tall black-and-green headwrap and a sharp dark tunic with green edging came walking out to meet us from where the steaming kettles puffed away near the back. "Abeeku," she said with a warm smile, "how are you doing? I have not seen you in a long time."

Boateng put a long arm around the short woman. "Mama Mawa, you are looking so beautiful today."

She had to look up to speak to him. "You come hungry?"

"Yes! Something smells wonderful."

"We are making red-red today."

"Ah, red-red! No wonder you are so busy, eh?"

"You come with me, I will get you a table near the girls."

She led us to a table that had a clear view of the kettles and the girls in bandanas preparing food. I felt awkward sitting in the little orange plastic chairs. They were so low to the ground they were like children's seats, putting us at eye-level with Mama Mawa. She wiped the table with a pink rag. "Just a few minutes, Abeeku," she said, sauntering away.

"Thank you, Mama. May we also have coffee, please."

A young girl came to the table with two hot paper cups, and the guards went to go stand at the outskirts of the dining area.

Boateng looked at me. I smiled as nicely as possible, but I was sure he could see my discomfort. "What do you think?" he asked.

"I like it," I said.

"Have you been to many internations, Mr. Borque?"

"Yes, many."

"And are you often taken on tours like this one?"

I could tell now that all this was not just for the sake of hospitality. He was making an obvious attempt to lead the conversation in a certain direction, but exactly where I didn't know yet. Up until then I'd been taken in by his friendliness, but I tried to remember the personality profile B&C had provided, the mention of his highly manipulative intelligence.

I made my voice more aloof, less earnest. "No."

"Usually your business does not extend beyond the financial districts and power centers of the internations you visit."

"That's correct."

"And why do you think that is?"

I took a sip of the coffee, which had been heavily sweetened and spiced. Boateng registered satisfaction at my lingering over the rich taste. "I don't know, Mr. Boateng. Why?"

He smiled broadly again and removed his hat. "If it is not too soon after your flight, I would like to discuss some business over our meal."

"Of course. I would very much like to discuss the particulars of the Fluorisaide deal with you. I had mentioned earlier that I hadn't seen an initial bid listed in the proposal."

"Forget about Fluorisaide for a moment. I would like to talk in a broader sense. You said that when you do business in other internations, they do not take you on tours of the cities or territories. Do you know why that is?"

I kept at the coffee.

"This, here," he said, motioning around us, "this is the reason. Because not all zones and internations are created equal in our World Organization. Perhaps in the North American Zone, or the Western European Zone, world culture has spread to every corner and has succeeded in remaking society, but most places in the world are just like it is right here in Ghana. World culture exists in the cities only near corporate headquarters or government centers. But away from those areas, you still have, and please forgive me for saying this, *countries*. Almost all of them with their original cultures partially intact."

I set my cup down. "Mr. Boateng, I feel I must remind you I'm simply a marketing relations executive. These things you're speaking of, they're far above what I've been deputized to discuss."

"I know who you are, Mr. Borque. I know the position you hold in your company, and I know what you have been sent here to do. I know you are to offer me Fluorisaide as a ploy to silence the overtures I've been making to the Board of Basil & Crittenden. The Fluorisaide deal was simply a way for me to get a representative—any representative—here in Ghana."

"Then perhaps you also know that my orders are to deflect any other propositions set forth by you."

"Indeed, and you will undoubtedly deflect them throughout the entirety of your stay. Nonetheless, you will still be obligated to report back to the Board after you have left Ghana, and they will be curious what it was I had to say. Then you will tell them for me." He crossed one leg over the other, totally at ease, picking up his cup and drinking from it in sips.

He was right. I had little else to do but listen.

"Now, I said I wanted to discuss business, but the truth is what I actually want to discuss is politics. You most likely know that corporations like my own are under strict mandates from the W.O. to provide certain services within their own internations. These can be anything from public utilities to peacekeeping to public works. This is not official, of course. Officially, the W.O. and its descending hierarchies of governing bodies are the ones who have the final say over such matters, but given the fact major multinationals and the W.O. are to some extent one and the same, it is not surprising to learn many bureaucratic tasks are handled by so-called 'private firms.' Are you following so far?"

"Yes."

"I am sure you know I became CEO of Kente by executive fiat, no?"

I nodded.

"I inherited from my predecessor vast responsibilities for the well-being of the Ghanaian people, not to mention many of the people in my general region of the African Zone." He smiled again for effect. "It would be extremely dangerous for you to ever tell anyone I told you this, but the responsibilities I inherited were so large, Mr. Borque, I began to question whether I was a businessman or a statesman. The reality is, I am both."

I looked around at the other tables, at these people who were so far from the boardrooms and meeting places of the corporate world, who took their meals in the street and spoke in happy, urgent voices. I never imagined I would hear something like this from a CEO while sitting at a plastic table out in public.

"Here in the African Zone," he continued, "our section of the economy is used by W.O. planners differently than where you are from, and as a result there is a difference in the way we live. We cannot say so openly because of world culture, but you can see for yourself that it is true. But for as different as you may find this, the gap between how it is here, in New Accra, the capital, and how it is in the rest of the internation is staggering, to say nothing of the rest of the zone. Although I can be arrested for saying it, I play a large role in the lives of these people, and after I inherited Kente and became acquainted with how the system works, I began to notice the more successful Kente is, which is merely another way of saying the more successful I am, the better things are for the people of Ghana, and for the people of our neighboring internations."

I couldn't help but note this conflation of his own well-being with the well-being of others. "I— I did read that you've been expanding aggressively. The quickest of any corporation in the world, at the moment."

"Yes. Some say too quickly, too aggressively. However, I say not quickly enough. And it is for this reason my reputation has become what it is. That I am a nationalist, a walking controversy, even megalomaniacal. But I ask you, if such responsibilities were weighing on your own shoulders, the fates of millions of people, how would you conduct business?"

He leveled an intense expression at me. Behind my amazement I wondered what it was he could possibly have in mind for B&C for him to be telling me all this.

Mama Mawa and the young waitress appeared at our table with the food. Each plate consisted of one whole cooked fish apiece, heads and tails still attached, even the eyeballs remaining, colorful mounds of red beans and vegetables. Boateng gave out a bellow of delight and fawned over Mama Mawa with a profuse, almost discomfiting gallantry before she left us to our meal.

"For now," he said, "let's set business aside. There will be plenty of time tomorrow. We will eat, and then take you to your hotel so you can rest."

I did my best to forget what he'd said, to put my mind back into my body there in the chop bar in Ghana.

Immediately after being dropped off at the hotel I fell asleep, not waking up until late in the morning the next day. I had slept almost twenty hours. The first thing I tried to do was reach Andrea, but her phone went to voicemail. I left a message with her secretary to remind her I was going to be meeting with Boateng later that afternoon, and to please call me back as soon as possible. I was scheduled to be at the Kente offices at 3:30, and by the time the front desk phoned to tell me the car had arrived I still hadn't received a call back from her. The whole thing was starting to frustrate me. Even if the Board was disinterested in Boateng's overtures to them, not sending a legal adviser to assist me was beginning to look almost like flat-out irresponsibility on Andrea's part. Before, I had been relieved just to have made it out of the hospital and through my psych eval, but it was starting to dawn on me how dangerous Boateng's outspoken nationalism could be to someone in my position. The last thing I needed was for another Roorback to slither out of the weeds and accuse me of backsliding into dissident ways. If that were to happen, especially on the heels of all this premorbid nonsense, B&C couldn't, or more likely just simply wouldn't, protect me.

The Kente skyscraper I was taken to in downtown New Accra was an adjunct building where Boateng kept his office. One of his dark-suited guards, who remained dead-faced and refused to be talkative, escorted me to the top floor. The secretary working in the inner office told me Boateng had left a message to let me know he was running a little late and wouldn't be there for another ten to fifteen minutes. The chairs in the waiting area faced a ten meter-long tropical fish aquarium set into the wall. The colorful bodies floated in lazy formations, soft music dissolving into the air like thin wisps of cobweb, but I was not calm. I was increasingly uncomfortable with the whole thing.

Time passed charmless and sterile until finally the secretary signaled to me from her desk.

"Mr. Borque, I just got word from Mr. Boateng that he has arrived at the building. He says you are welcome to wait for him in his office."

I gathered up my bag and thanked her, twisting the gold handle and pushing open the heavy door. Boateng's office was immense. After closing the door behind me I couldn't help pausing at the threshold to overview it. The walls were paneled with a rich wood that blushed resin-red. Above, a high ceiling dripped with glossy white carvings resembling beehives. The main area of the floor was sunken down half a meter with a raised walkway lining it on all sides, accentuated by a trim black handrail made of twisted, textured iron. The whole south wall was one expansive window, showing the spires and sprawl of New Accra and letting in a voluminous natural light. Striping the other three walls were long rows of brightly-colored, modern-looking books that seemingly hovered on near-invisible shelves. At the center of the office was a desk the size of a small boat topped with maroon leather and black slate, and overhanging it a gargantuan metal ceiling fan painted a smooth matte-black, the wingspan of its four oversized blades covering a full two-thirds of the entire ceiling space. The effect of the room was so strong it was like entering some baroque institutional chamber, a feeling at once both public and private. I descended into the main pit of the room and took a seat in one of the heavy cushioned chairs facing the desk.

Almost as soon as I did, Boateng burst through the doors behind me in his own personal outsized manner, clad in a finely fitting pinstripe suit and puffing at a nub of cigar. He extended his arms to both sides with a briefcase hanging from his right hand and bounded toward his desk with an athletic, busy stride. His seeming good cheer was set at such a deliriously high level it came off as practically threatening. "Mr. Borque, I am so sorry to keep you waiting, I am just returning from dealing with some other matters. But no matter, I am here now. Well!—what do you think of my office?"

"It's..." I looked all around the impressive room.

"Yes, it's exquisite, no? I must say I am proud of it. I helped with the design, even with the construction in some areas. So"—he slapped the briefcase down, seating himself on the desk's edge—"I am here, and we can commence with business." He tugged at the cuffs of his shirt peeking through the sleeves of his suit coat.

"Yes, well," I began. "I took the liberty of filling in an initial price on your Fluorisaide proposal. I'm guessing from your comments yesterday that you'll find it fair."

"Of course, of course."

"Beyond that, I suppose I'm here mainly at your bidding."

"Indeed, you are right. So I will not waste your time." He stood up off the desk and began to pace behind it, arms folded with concentration. He turned and considered the view through the window, which from our angle at the desk was only clear sky. "I am going to be blunt with you," he said. "I have expanded Kente's profits as much as possible here in the western region of the African Zone, and this gives me tremendous power over my own internation, but there are still limits to that power. Have you heard of the Nigerian conglomerate Alaafia?"

"No."

He paced. "They are the second-largest corporation on the continent, even though they are very far behind Kente in terms of size and power. Still, this fact does not insulate me from their influence, especially when it comes to their environmental engineering capabilities, an area in which my own company is weak." He pulled an ashtray from one of the drawers of the desk and stubbed out his cigar with kingly anxiety, in the same motion taking another full cigar and cutter from his breast pocket. "I do not see eye-to-eye with Alaafia's CEO. Our proximity to one another makes us familiar business partners, but Machie Obode and I are not only rival oligarchs. We have developed a personal enmity between us. I find her cynical and self-serving, while she considers me to be a hypocrite with warped beliefs. What I can say of this is, at least with my warped beliefs I act honorably towards her, whereas she delights in sabotaging my efforts, and in the process makes things unpleasant for my people."

My earlier frustration with the situation was now building close to outright anger, not necessarily at Boateng or even at one thing in particular, but more at the sum total of the recent convergence of circumstances in my own life. I felt I had escaped one situation that posed a threat to my job and mental health status only to be placed in another that fed into the false narrative of my political subversion. I was developing the sense these things were somehow out of my control.

Boateng continued while lighting the cigar in haste. "Ghana has been one of the least affected internations in the world by the environmental crisis. Our sole major revitalization project has focused on our extensive river system, an important natural asset that provides for all Ghanaians. Machie's newest move in her campaign to antagonize me has been to attempt to acquire a contract with the W.O. to develop a model for sustainable resource extraction from our rivers. This I cannot let her do. I know her true intentions, which will be to exploit Ghana's environmental riches even as she allegedly works to revitalize them. But I am limited in my means to stop her because Kente, with its current engineering program, is unable to compete with Alaafia for the government contract. To make matters worse, Machie is being aided with substantial outside investment from your own company."

I interrupted his speech, hearing myself becoming hot under the collar. "Mr. Boateng, if I may."

He stopped.

I searched for the correct wording that might restrain my agitation. "Not that I don't appreciate your candor, but what is the point of telling me these things? In the first place, you must be aware I'll be completely unable to relay any of this information to my superiors because, I would remind you, I'm not much more than a functionary within Basil & Crittenden, and saying any of this would likely get me fired, if not arrested. Secondly, I don't doubt you have knowledge of my own personal background, which includes a conviction of lower treason. None of these details will help you get whatever it is you want, and they pose a danger to me, so why not simply tell me what your offer to the Board is?"

He was unfazed by my outburst. "I tell you these things so you may understand the situation you are in. I do have knowledge of who you are, and I do not know why B&C would send you to conduct this business, even just to act as a messenger, but whatever the reason you are here instead of someone else, it does not change the fact that, for the time being, you are my go-between with your Board."

He had vindicated the suspicion that my being there was not normal, and I grew self-defensive out of a sudden feeling of dread. "Then I must insist you get to the point without going into any more detail."

He narrowed his eyes, losing some of his patience with my tone. He walked around to the front of the desk and stood in front of where I sat, ashy-sweet smoke enveloping my nose. "I cannot do that." The friendliness in his voice changed into something ruthless, unsparing. "As you say, your job is as a functionary. I am the CEO of the largest corporation on this continent, and I did not rise to what I am today, from my own previous position as a functionary, by being dense. I do not mean you harm, but you have nonetheless been put into a position exceeding your pay grade. I am aware that to you this must seem a strange way to be speaking in a professional setting, but at this echelon of business one deals in truths, even if they are unpleasant or dangerous, and what I am telling you may indeed help you. So you will understand if I must go on against your wishes."

I kept my mouth shut. If I knew anything it was that I couldn't dictate terms to someone like him.

He resumed his pacing on the other side of the table, launching back into his explanation. "Now, to oppose Alaafia's efforts to take control of Ghana's river systems, I am forced to look for a substantial injection of capital to develop my own environmental engineering sector at the necessary speed. The only way I am able to do this is to offer Basil & Crittenden a better, more favorable contract than my competition. To obtain this commitment from your Board, I am willing to offer in exchange the exclusive rights to develop and exploit a small but significant percentage of some of Ghana's most fertile, productive lands, as well as a uniquely favorable interest rate on any loans made. And finally, I am also offering the Board a special one-time gift." He approached the desk and laid two hands gingerly atop the briefcase he had been carrying when he arrived, indicating the gift was contained therein.

He must have seen I was in a state of minor terror because his expression softened. He sat down in a fatherly manner in his own magnificent seat. He laced his fingers together in silence, the cigar swiveled to one side of his mouth. A wise old potted bonsai tree sat to one side of the desk, making him appear philosophical behind its meditative aura. The friendly tone returned. "Mr. Borque, like you, my reputation suffers from accusations not altogether accurate. I am deemed an ultra-nationalist bogeyman by the W.O. and my competitors because of my opinions, and although I am mostly exempt from psych evals as a CEO, I have been officially classified as exhibiting megalomaniacal tendencies. No matter, I am far from the only one to ever be misdiagnosed by evaluators for corrupt reasons. But I must tell you, I am not power-mad like they say. I seek power for far more pragmatic reasons than to merely satisfy my own delusions. No, I seek power because our world, our system, is not perfect, but I have been anointed into a post that allows me to manipulate outcomes, and long ago I promised myself I would manipulate them for the benefit of not just my own people, but for the benefit of all the people of Afri—"

Just then a startling cracking sound cut off his sentence, like wooden boards being snapped apart, and underneath that an even more alarming metal squeal, like pipes being wrenched and bent in all directions. Boateng's eyes grew wide. He looked around in confusion, taking the cigar from his mouth, smoke still seeping from the spaces between his top teeth like carbon fumes from the barrel of a recently-fired gun.

"What the hell was that?" he said.

The cracking sound returned in full force and Boateng looked up just before something came crashing down on top of him and the desk, causing him to vanish beneath it in a blink and the desk to shatter on one side into a burst of splinters and pieces. I screamed and threw my arms up over my face, hearing a sound so putrid it made my bones go numb. After the impact there were the noises of debris clattering and dusting to the floor, then it was quiet. I let my arms down slowly, my whole face quivering with adrenaline and my breath escaping through my nose in shivering spurts like I was in freezing weather. I saw, in utter stupefaction, that what had fallen was the oversized ceiling fan. The center motor was collapsed in a crooked heap through the desk, and there was no sign of Boateng. His chair had been knocked over—I could just see some of its carvings extending above the wreckage. To either side of me were two of the fan's huge blades, sticking up where they had missed me by only a meter in both directions. I felt a spot of something just under my eye. I put a hand to it and saw on the tip of my middle finger the tiniest smear of blood. Not my own.

I jolted up from my seat in a panic so bad I was afraid I might be going into shock. Directly above was a huge tear in the high ceiling where the fan had detached. With a shambling gait I ducked beneath one of the tilted blades—longer and wider than a bartop—and went around the desk to see what had happened to Boateng. A slowly-rising scream that began as a moan rose out of me as his body came into view. He had been gruesomely crushed to death. My own shaking hand slapped up against my mouth and I turned away, sinking down to my haunches on the floor. I crawled as far away from the desk as possible until I was sitting up against the wall with my eyes closed. I felt tears rising as vivid memories of the pistol shot that had killed my father flooded into my senses, seeming to transport me back in time.

I sat on the floor until I had recovered to a workable emotional pitch, and it was only then I realized just how strange it was that no one had come into the office. The noise of the fan and my yelling couldn't possibly have gone unnoticed by Boateng's secretary, or maybe the office was so soundproof she hadn't heard a thing. I also couldn't imagine there weren't any security devices or surveillance cameras, but nonetheless there I was, sitting alone in the room with Boateng's mangled corpse. None of his dark-suited guards bursting in. Not even the slightest noise. The window still showed the calm blue sky outside. I had no idea what would happen when somebody did come in and discover the situation, if maybe I would be blamed for some reason. I doubted it. The evidence of the accident seemed perfectly clear, but the longer I waited for something to happen the more irrational my thoughts became. I looked back toward the desk and something on the floor caught my eye. There was a large scattering of paper money mixed into the broken pieces of desk and ceiling. Curiosity pulled me to my feet, and taking extreme care not to look in the direction of the body I stepped to an angle where I could get a better view.

The briefcase had been knocked to the floor and broken in half, tangled piles of world scrips reaming from it in a violent arc. The amount, it was obvious to see, was astronomical—Boateng's one-time gift to the Board to get them to abandon investment in Alaafia and redirect it to him. I shook my head in disbelief and returned to my corner, deciding I would sit there until someone came in.

But no one did. Minutes passed and I finally couldn't wait any longer. If I did they would wonder why I hadn't alerted anyone. I went to the doors and stepped into the inner office. The ghostly music and drifting fish formations were just as before, but the desk where the secretary had been was now abandoned. I walked farther in, looking everywhere for where she might be. Nobody. I stepped out into the hallway where I had left the dark-suited man who had escorted me standing by the elevator. There were bathrooms on either end of the corridor. I went to the women's first and knocked loudly, calling out if anyone was there. When no answer came I stepped inside and called out again, looking under the stall door for feet. The secretary was gone. I went to the men's bathroom and again found nobody.

Back in the inner office I screamed out. "Anyone!"

I swung open the office door and stood there, observing the ghastly scene from afar. A far-reaching moat of blood had formed around the base of the desk, revealing that the floor sloped slightly toward the entrance. The money remained splayed out.

Something was definitely going on. It couldn't be that everyone had just disappeared by coincidence. I looked at the time on my mobile and guessed it had been almost half an hour since Boateng had been killed by the fan. An eel of paranoia emerged from the fathoms of my mind and extended itself through my body. I started calling everything into question. For what reason would someone want Boateng dead, and for me to be left alone with him? Possibilities skittered through my head at a dizzying pace, but nothing seemed logical, or, if it was logical, there was no way for me to know why. More time passed, until I'd been standing there for forty-five minutes without anyone showing up.

I pushed everything out of my head and rushed to some quick conclusions. There was no way this had happened on accident; for some reason everyone had left, or had been removed; if both those things were the case, it seemed likely something bad was about to happen to me. The only option I had was to leave. Maybe that was what whoever had done this wanted me to do. But even if there weren't security cameras in Boateng's office they were definitely everywhere else, meaning I was implicated no matter what. Someone was watching me even at that very moment. A terrible understanding filled my head: this was going to be the end of me. Whether I ended up dead or incarcerated was probably just splitting hairs.

My only thought was escape. I rushed into the office, scooped up handfuls of scrips that hadn't been soaked through with blood, stuffed them in the bag still slung across my waist, and ran back to the hallway. I called the elevator and the doors opened immediately. I jammed the button for the lobby. When I reached the ground floor the cavernous main entrance was revealed. I took a deep breath and walked out as calmly as possible, but there was no longer a receptionist at the front desk, no security guard, no one at all. I fled through the glass doors. Beyond the building's plaza there was a steady stream of traffic on the street, people in business clothes walking the sidewalks. I went to the corner and flagged down one of the infinite red taxis passing by. It had seemed like the whole building was deserted. Nobody had tried to stop me. The taxi made it to my hotel and I went up to my room, all my things just where I had left them. I stood there rubbing my eyes when my mobile shrieked to life in my pocket and nearly caused me to jump out of my skin.

It was a message from Andrea.

Stanly, I hope the business with Boateng is concluded. I haven't heard from you in a while, and I can't be sure if you've been checking your messages. We need you back in New Boston as soon as possible. The clearance on your psych eval expired already. They're calling you back in for a second opinion. I'm not sure what's going on but it doesn't sound good.

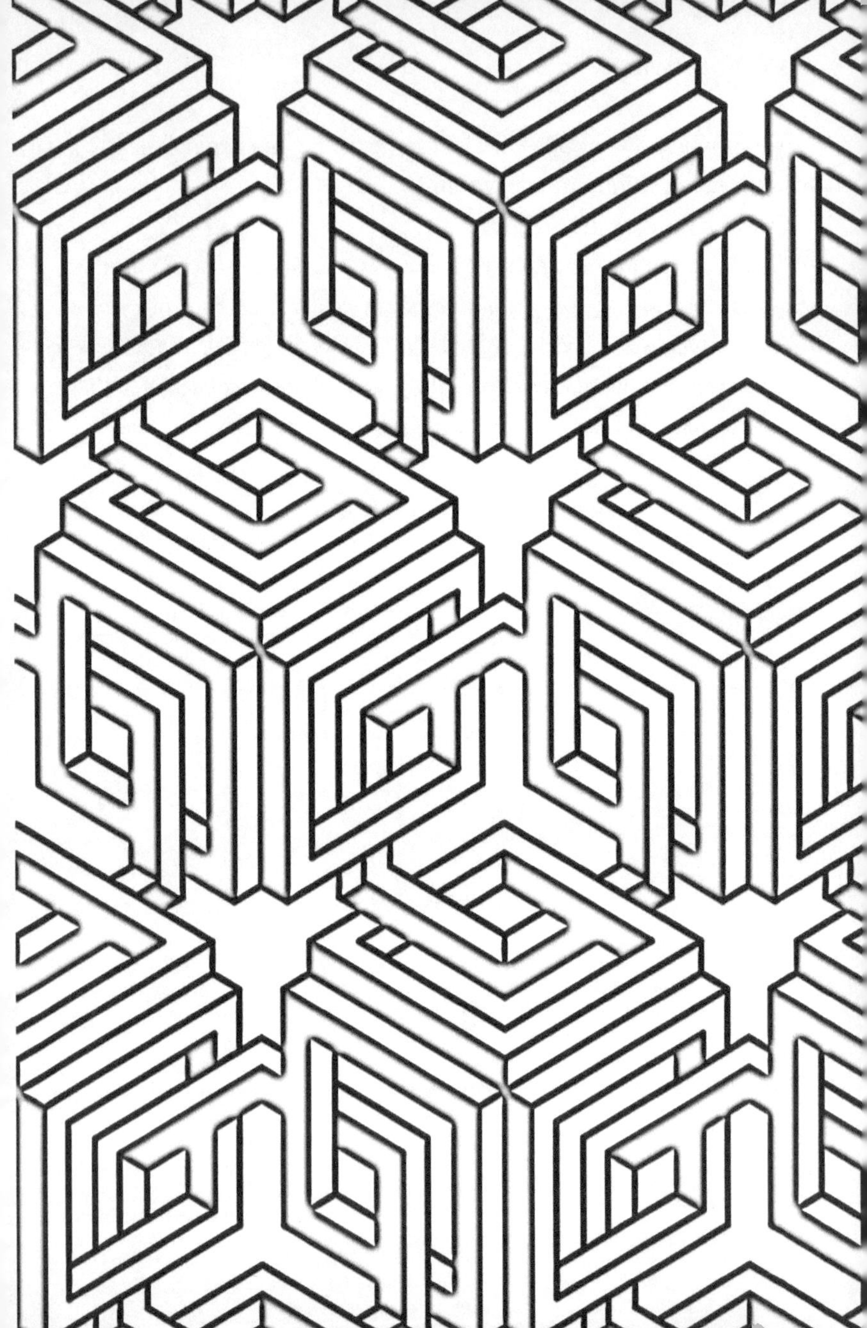

MORBID

At first I planned to run, to start moving and not stop. Then I realized there was nowhere to go. There was nowhere I could run to where they couldn't follow me, couldn't find me, wouldn't be looking for me. There was not the slightest chance of evading a globally-integrated surveillance network. There was no way to change my identity, or if there was I had no idea how to go about doing it, and I would be caught well before figuring it out. I didn't know what was happening, or what I was caught up in, but eventually I decided the only thing I could do was to fly back to New Boston and report to my psych eval. When my mother was arrested for her IFA activities and my father and I were arrested immediately afterwards, the only thing we could do was tell the authorities we hadn't done anything wrong, which was true. The same thing applied here. I hadn't killed Boateng. I had only witnessed it. The only thing I was guilty of was stealing some money in a moment of great emotional stress and paranoia.

When I took the time to count the cash, I gave up after only a few minutes. There was too much. The total amount was probably a million scrips, if not more. "Some" money amounted to a major robbery.

Either way, it didn't matter anymore. Maybe it was best not to even get on a plane before calling Andrea to tell her everything. Boateng's proposal, the ceiling fan, how the building had become inexplicably empty, and especially about the money. There was no way all this wouldn't be found out. Someone was going to discover Boateng's body, then the whole thing was going to turn into headline news. If I didn't tell someone soon, I was going to make everything worse for myself.

I picked up my mobile from the bed and dialed her. The rings went on and on without ever going to voicemail. I tried her secretary's number but she didn't answer either. That had never happened before. I tried calling several more times, feeling progressively more certain, no matter how unreal it seemed, that all of this was by design. I didn't even bother to send her a message. The whole thing was impossible. She claimed in her text she hadn't heard from me, but I had told her secretary just that morning to have her call my phone.

I spent the entire night deliberating what to do, pacing the hotel room and fluctuating between total hysteria and cool fatalism, waiting for anything to happen. I kept the news on, expecting to see the story break, but there was no trace of it, no hint it had ever even happened. A strong desire emerged to tell myself I was losing my mind, that I could have the luxury of not believing any of this, but I knew exactly what I had seen. By morning I hadn't slept, and hadn't been able to come up with any foolproof course of action. My return flight was leaving in only a few hours. If I was going to be framed, arrested, killed, or whatever, why hadn't it happened yet? I would go back and tell Andrea everything in person. I just didn't know what else to do.

Boarding the plane for the extremely long trip home, my fear was that I would spend the whole time worrying about everything just as I had in the hotel room. Instead I ended up sleeping even harder than the first time. The plane ride and even the layover in

Sucre all fuzzed together into one long dreamless blur, broken up into awful moments of wakefulness in which I would remember what was going on and in protest fall back into unconsciousness. I couldn't escape the thought that this unwillingness to stay awake was a product of the famous passivity my mother always scolded me for. Her opinion was that I accepted the way things were too readily, that I would rather go with the flow than fight to improve my own circumstances. I purged my mind of my own voice. At least in prison I would be able to sleep.

As soon as I touched down in New Boston I called Andrea again. I was hoping to speak to her before having to report to my psych eval later in the day. Again there was no answer. I waited nervously in baggage claim for the suitcase containing the money. The black bag spit out onto the carousel like a reminder of a death sentence. Forlorn, I went to catch a taxi to the evaluation site.

The driver saw the address I requested and clicked his tongue in sympathy. The site was located in an auxiliary building within a W.O. administrative plaza, the usual steady flow of people trafficking the area around it. All Department of Mental Health Evaluation facilities kept up the appearance of being vaguely medical. The interior resembled a doctor's office rather than a bureaucratic complex full of World Org minders, the people in the crowded fourth floor waiting room looking as distressed and irritated as ever. I checked in at the desk and chose an empty seat, arranging my bags in front of me so they wouldn't take up too much room in expectation of waiting the usual hour or two past my appointment time, but almost as soon as I sat down the receptionist came out and called my name.

"Borque, Stanly?"

The people who had seen me arrive turned to stare, sensing something wasn't normal.

The receptionist led me through the tangled complex of indistinguishable hallways and doors, finally stopping at one and holding it open for me. The room was antiseptic white, containing a grey couch, a chair, and an industrial cabinet.

"Okay, here you go, and Evlt. Kasza will be right with you, sir."

"Thank you." My voice was shaking. Even though I felt resigned, it didn't erase the fear.

The evaluator came in several minutes later looking hurried. She had pinned back red hair and kept both hands on her tablet most of the time, giving the impression she could play it at a virtuoso level. While greeting me she wore a grimace of concentration, her body language artful in a cold, gliding way. The recording equipment was already set up by her chair and she gave me the standard declaration of my rights. I acknowledged them, holding my hands together in my lap and eyeing the suitcase sitting to my left holding a million scrips worth of cash inside.

Her fingers danced across the instrument. "All right, sir, to get right to the point. The reason you've been called back for a second opinion is because you were recently evaluated by James Roorback during a stay at New Boston Central. The results of that evaluation stated you were exhibiting symptoms of BPD premorbidity with risks of advancement to a morbid phase."

I was sweating.

"You just returned from a business trip, correct?"

"Y— excuse me, sorry. Yes."

"We received a claim from your employer informing us they hadn't heard from you in four days, that you weren't responding to calls or messages."

"No," I said, "that's not true. I was in contact with my section supervisor Andrea Valle. As a matter of fact, it was the other way around. She fell out of contact with *me*."

"That's not what your employer is claiming."

"Maybe there was a technical error, then. I would be happy to show you the records on my mobile."

"That's not necessary, sir, but even so, phone records don't constitute an official entry in your file unless we were to conduct a warranted search."

"Well, at least just to show you I'm not lying." I was digging in my pocket for my phone.

She put a hand up to stop me. "Sir, sir, please. Whatever doesn't constitute an official method of data capture is illegal for me to base my evaluation on. I'll make a note that you're disputing your employer's claim, so make sure not to delete any records you plan on submitting as evidence."

"Okay," I said, sinking back against the couch and leaning my forehead into my hand in suppressed misery.

"It looks like Evlt. Roorback also upped your dosage of Pentaf-alex. Have you been sticking to it?"

"Yes, ma'am."

She marked something down on the tablet. "So, you're claiming your employer actually fell out of contact with you while you were abroad in India, not the other way around."

"Ghana."

"Excuse me?"

"I was abroad in Ghana, not India. I was supposed to go to India, but I came down with a case of food poisoning that put me in the hospital. They reassigned me."

She shot me a sidelong look, as if I were saying something suspicious. "Sir, your employer's claim very clearly states that you were abroad in India. I don't think Basil & Crittenden would make that kind of clerical mistake."

"But it's true. I can prove it. I have documentation on my mobile, I even have my plane ticket still here with me."

"Sir, again—"

"I mean, look, I have it right here." I was unzipping my work bag to fish out the boarding pass.

"*Sir.* Now I've already told you this once, I cannot accept warrantless pieces of documentation for official file entry. Whatever evidence you have to dispute your employer's claim will have to be submitted through an attorney, which I am not."

For as many times as I'd been evaluated in my life, which was more than the average person, I had never heard of "official" methods of data capture or "warrantless" documentation. Evaluators normally dug into your personal information with little to no concern for any kind of procedure, including your phone. Something was obviously conspiring against me here, but I couldn't figure out who, or especially why. Most likely it wouldn't matter very soon. I could sit there and dispute the false information provided in the claim, but aside from that I was defenseless, and I tried to start getting myself used to the idea that I was bound for a psych facility by the end of the eval. Evlt. Kasza proceeded to question what kind of business I believed I was conducting for B&C out in Ghana rather than India, and why it was I believed my employer had made such a grave error, or why, if what I said was true, they were so concerned by my behavior that they felt it necessary to file a claim. I simply told her I didn't know, that I had been sent to Ghana to meet with the CEO of Kente, Inc. about a routine product bid.

"And who else accompanied you on this trip?" she asked.

"No one. They sent me by myself."

"So you mean to tell me you were sent on an overseas business negotiation to speak directly with a corporate CEO without even one other member of personnel? I'm sorry, sir, but this is beginning to seem a bit far-fetched."

I couldn't say anything. She was right. The fact that they would have sent me alone on such an assignment was completely unbelievable. I became lightheaded.

"I don't think there's much need to continue. After reviewing your employer's claim and Evlt. Roorback's report, it seems apparent to me that your BPD has entered a morbid phase."

My stomach dropped, and I braced myself for the bad news.

"I've seen this kind of bending of the truth and even disjunction with reality many times in the past, and though it's a product of your sickness, it still requires me to change your classification and to recommend you to a psych facility. Once there you'll be able to contact your attorney and prepare a case for your defense."

So the worst was true. I felt like I might cry. "I understand," I managed to say through watering eyes, just wanting it to be over.

"You'll have to forgive the inconvenience, but I'm going to need time to submit your employer's claim and the transcript of this recording to get your admission approved. You'll be required to wait here until that time. There's an intercom on the wall. If you need to use the restroom or anything else, use it to page a nurse and they'll help you, but beyond that you're not to leave this room for any reason. Afterwards we'll move you straight into processing. Do you understand?"

I nodded.

"Good. If you'll excuse me." She tucked her tablet underneath her arm and marched out of the room.

Even through my despondency, this last part struck me as curious. People got hauled off to psych facilities all the time for the most minor of reasons, and never had I heard of an evaluator needing, much less getting, approval to do so. This was all too much to handle. Ever since seeing my mother get sent to prison I'd had a fear of incarceration worse than death, and that was now shortly to become my exact future. All those years I'd spent trying to better myself in spite of everything that had happened, trying to work hard and fly under the radar, all gone.

My eyes landed on my suitcase.

Unless I ran. But that was a crazy thought, there was so much surveillance in the building it would be pointless to try. Not that surveillance had stopped me from leaving the Kente offices in Ghana and flying halfway around the world. Still, the impulse was insane.

I leaned my head back against the couch, waiting.

I supposed things couldn't really get much worse, but the idea of them getting any worse at all was intimidating. And yet I wondered why I should have been allowed to witness Boateng's death and flee the African Zone only to be called back to New Boston so I could be tossed in a psych facility. No mention of any of this in the news, no one saying anything about it to me, as if the whole thing had never happened. Maybe I was being arrogant to think I could know, but there seemed to be no higher reasoning behind it whatsoever.

Most people, once sent to a psych facility, never came back. Or at least not for a very long time.

I stood up, went to the door. It was unlocked. I looked back at the suitcase, frozen with fear. I couldn't believe I was considering doing what I felt like I was about to—but I had to ask myself, why would they leave me alone in here? Surveillance or no, if this were actually standard procedure people would run all the time.

I grabbed the suitcase and eased the door open. There was distant noise, but nobody in the hallway. I stepped out, looked up at the ceiling. In the far corner at the end of the hall was a small opaque orb, like one eye amongst many on the face of an enigmatic, all-seeing spider. I waited, expecting someone to appear. Then I walked. I followed the path I had taken back to the fourth floor waiting room. Holding my breath, I swung open the door and took the straightest route to the elevator, making sure not to look back. I punched the call button, then changed my mind and took the stairwell. No voices shouting for me to stop, no hand on my shoulder, no alarms. I beelined through the lobby to the main doors, stepped out into the bright afternoon. For a brief moment I paused to cast a glance back at the building, baffled once again. A few moments later I was in a taxi.

I knew it wasn't necessary to flee because if the W.O. and DMHE weren't intentionally permitting me to escape then I would have been in a psych facility already. But something deeply instinctual took over my decision-making process and told me to get out, move, run away. Apparently my brain could know the entire globe was controlled by a single government with unified objectives but couldn't accept the knowledge as true now that it meant my downfall. That same gut-level impulse had taken over when I had made the decision in Boateng's office to take the money. The only thing to do was to stop thinking so much and give in to myself. Not because I expected to avoid my fate. More because I was starting to understand that it didn't matter what I did.

I went to Uruguay first, latching onto the idea to zig-zag north and south across the equator. The money, hypothetically, could last me forever. Something my father had said just before he died kept coming to mind.

Things really are different now. There's no way to change anything, we can't control what happens to us. We get to go on living, but for what?

I'd never thought much about what he said that day because I had always known what I thought about the world. Watching my mother be sentenced to life in prison just because she didn't agree with the government had had an impact on me. For such a broad reason, she gave up her entire life. The thought of that haunted me walking in the balmy weather of Montevideo, that my mother was still existing somewhere, but at the same time was as good as dead. She could never be there with me, looking at the sky, deciding what to eat later, drinking a glass of beer in a bar or having a conversation with someone new. I hadn't had sympathy for some of my father's sufferings, either, because when he was forced to give up his directorship at Logan-Barr for long hours working in a dish pit, I had thought to myself, *at least you're free.* I understood his melancholy over the loss of my mother, but in a perverse way I had thought, *you can still find someone new.* From a young age, my only ambition in life had been to stay out of trouble, to remain free.

After only a few days I caught a flight to Spain, crossing the equator again. Lying in bed in a luxury suite in Barcelona, I began to wonder if my idea of freedom had been as smart as I'd presumed it was for so long. My mother had a very specific conception of freedom, namely that it no longer existed. Her thinking was that freedom was the invention of a particular epoch of history. It had not always been the case that peoples' every action and daily lives were recorded and stored and coerced. Examples could be found in history of attempts at such total control, but she said that, for a very distinct time period, the methods of control available to authorities to exercise over people was limited, at least in comparison to the present day. Freedom, her argument went, actually did exist back then because not only did people have a substantial amount of anonymity, they also had an infinite amount of different identities to choose from, and with those identities came goals, aspirations, reasons for personal being, along with the darker aspects, much publicized by world culture propaganda, like war, exclusion, racism, clashes of belief systems. She was of the opinion—and to me this always seemed the part that was overly vague—that freedom no longer existed because there was no longer any choice of politics, or open fields of artistic and intellectual expression, and especially no confidentiality of personhood. *Okay*, I always thought when she would go on at length during my home lessons, which in retrospect I realized had the intent of molding me into her own distinct brand of subversive, *but what about the freedom to be happy? To choose to be content?*

When I enrolled in New Boston Polytechnic, I didn't do so with the expectation I would become something as relatively successful as Head of Cultural Marketing Relations for one of the North American Zone's wealthiest corporations. I chose to do it for myself, no matter what the outcome turned out to be. I had the simple ambition of participating in the world. I always considered my father's suicide, at its heart, as the product of his inability to come to terms with the erasure of his old life and his reduction in social stature. I found those reasons superficial, inexcusable. Was there nothing else to live for in this world besides one's job title and personal circumstances? Why not be happy with what he still had, especially when his wife, my mother, sat rotting in a cell. I questioned what my own importance to him had been, if he had even seen me as a factor in whether or not to pull the trigger during those final moments. Were his reasons for killing himself really good enough?

As for me, I tried to follow a different path. I never got myself embroiled in political questions, either at work or in my personal life. Things that even most people griped about, like psych evals or corporate corruption, I accepted as being just part of life and stayed silent. After getting hired at B&C, I worked hard. I never thought I would be promoted, never asked for it. I was perfectly happy to live within my means. I didn't go out at night, didn't look for friends or a relationship. What I had wanted, ever since a young age, was my own sense of peace.

I left Spain and flew into New Hanoi. The city there was a sterling model of world culture. Very little of the old Vietnamese character remained in its yawning thoroughfares and uniform structures. Near my hotel there was a cafe with a patio where I ate breakfast. I watched the people and thought to myself that, aside from the morphological differences, they looked absolutely no different from the people I had just seen in Spain, or in Uruguay. The cafe I was eating at—the same business existed in both those internations, not to mention New Boston and Ghana as well. I had never cared before, but suddenly all this sameness did start to strike me as such a loss, an enforced sham that made a person go brain-dead. There was no wonder in it, nothing really alive. My mother would have been proud of my thoughts. A twinge of loneliness played through my chest, and I stole a quick look at a beautiful woman sitting by herself three tables away who reminded me of how the women looked in Ghana. She had braids reaching to her collarbone and wore a trim black jumpsuit, reading on her mobile with a mug of coffee close at hand. For a fleeting moment I wanted to go talk to her.

The World Org had its own take on why it existed. The kind of stuff they taught you in school and the documentaries they disseminated all followed the same formula. Images of cities slowly being engulfed by saltwater floods, bombs exploding and crowds running in terror, brief snapshots of skeletal people, dead forests, empty supermarket shelves, tidal waves toppling buildings, the Eiffel Tower encased in a shell of arctic ice, dry lake beds and people unable to go out in the sun without protective gear and certain land masses being erased from the map. Then old scenes from the final summit in which the Delegation of Nations brought the World Organization into existence, closeups of certain famous, long-dead leaders applauding. A global government supposedly formed out of the necessity to save the human species.

My mother's version was different. According to her, during the time period leading up to the Delegation of Nations the world had finished its transformation into a collection of nation-states that all practiced total social surveillance, leading to a wave of de facto authoritarian regimes the people were no longer able to unseat. Those who had the real power, whom she called the "global elite," the ones with all the money who had become capitalist-politician hybrids over the previous fifty years, had waited to act until the planet descended into irreversible crisis because they finally realized not even they would be exempt from the horrors of ecological collapse. Becoming one unified Delegation of Nations already foreshadowed the route the countries would have to take, and since all governments had turned into surveillance states anyway, and since no potentate could any longer be removed from power through either foreign or domestic force, merging the world's sovereignties into one continuous body under the rule of a Supreme

Executive Congress just seemed to make good sense. The tricky part was how to get the members of the world's ultra-rich class who did not hold political office to go along with this enshrinement of power. The solution—a lazy one by my mother's estimation—came in the decision to integrate all markets into one giant command economy, painstakingly dividing up corporate assets into a hierarchical, oligarchical system. Some wiggle-room aside, the rulers would simply be the rulers, not subject to the scrutiny of the people. Theoretically, this would streamline all available resources into solving the world's environmental problems.

Which, to some undeniable extent, it had. But not without consequences. The first of those consequences became the most important event in recent world history, even more important than the creation of the W.O. itself. Adding to the massive death tolls stacking up due to all kinds of reasons, not least of which was a rash of new and more resilient diseases, came the inexplicable phenomenon of a pandemic outbreak of suicides. More than a tenth of the world's population ended their own lives during a twenty-year time period, over 800 million deaths. The breakdown generation was my grandparents' generation, and its effects also filtered into that of my parents, the second breakdown generation. Like most things, my mother had her own theory for why it happened. People were resistant at first to the so-called "left-wing revolution" of the World Org. Not only were they suffering through an impossibly bleak present, they were now faced with a monolithic totalitarianism about which they could do nothing. Freedom, both personal and political, had officially died. Further proof of this point, in her mind, was the fact that the W.O. was quick to exploit the pandemic, stoking fears by blaming it on "widespread mental disease," leading to the formation of the DMHE and mandatory psych evals for all citizens. Now, long after the suicide rates had dropped off to nearly pre-pandemic levels, the government had a convenient tool for thought control and oppression.

These were all things I knew, but had never much cared about. To me, they were always just the dry facts of a history lesson I didn't consider to be of much use to me in my own personal life. It was my mother's axe to grind, not mine. Thinking about them now, I didn't feel empowered or revolutionary. I felt hopeless.

I was on the move again, this time to Australia. A little over two weeks had passed since I had absconded with Boateng's bribe money from the psych eval site in New Boston and still nothing had happened to me. There was no news of Boateng's death, or stolen money, or a fugitive BPD patient from New Boston, or anything relating to my situation, and finally I stopped my daily routine of scouring the headlines. I tried to relax, to enjoy the indoor city of New Sydney.

I stayed at the same hotel I'd stayed at in New Hanoi and went to the same nearby cafe. The sun shield radiated down a mellow daytime brightness and again I watched the people passing in front of the patio. I ate the exact same thing I had in New Hanoi. Again, the people were similar. Every movement tracked and recorded. Every place the same. No options except the ones put directly in front of you.

On the other hand, my mother had her moments when she dabbled in conservative opinions.

I guess when it comes down to it we're nothing but the victims of our own advancements. Governments had no choice but to keep up with the technological innovations of their own citizens, so no wonder surveillance turned into the norm. Add environmental devastation into the picture and there really weren't any good choices left for humankind. Some kind of agenda had to be set. I don't agree with it, but the challenges were real.

I looked around half-expecting to see the same Ghanaian-looking woman sitting a few tables down from me. Maybe I would talk to her this time, but there were no familiar faces.

My own sense of happiness hadn't been affected by dry facts before, but for the first time I felt like I was possibly starting to understand some of the things I had never been able to. I was starting to think my mother had been right that freedom—including my own personal sense of freedom to be content with myself and my life—was a dead concept. I didn't understand what was happening to me, but it was happening in spite of how committed I'd always been to staying out of arguments, politics, competition. No matter how agreeable I was, no matter how little I made waves, it hadn't saved me from being wrongfully convicted of a felony, or from being classified with a mental disorder I didn't actually have. Now it hadn't saved me from getting caught up in something that was clearly bigger than I knew and being condemned by my own employer. My father may really *have* had sufficient reasons for killing himself, reasons no better or worse than the 800 million people who had done it before him. No one could control what was happening to them. The world falling apart into a wheezing, polluted disaster of cataclysmic proportions, and the only way to save themselves was to bow down and kiss the boots of those who had caused the crisis in the first place. We got to go on living, but for what exactly? The answer wasn't clear. Reality itself was at odds with the human spirit.

I felt a hand come down and squeeze my shoulder.

I twisted in my seat and saw the woman from the cafe in New Hanoi standing over me. She wore the same black jumpsuit, a resolutely dour expression framed by her falling braids. Her eyes burned into mine.

"Stanly," she said, in a Ghanaian accent.

"Please don't be scared," she said. "May I sit down?"

I was scared. Out of my mind, in fact, but I could do nothing but acquiesce.

She took a seat at the table. Now that I was seeing her at close range, I realized she was taller and larger than me. A broad white shirt collar rose out of the neck of her black jumpsuit, and despite her stature her face was an elegant circular shape. She propped her elbows in front of her, saying in a tone of voice calmer than distant thunder, "You must relax, I am not here to hurt you. My name is Emma. I am a friend."

"A friend? Who are you? I saw you in New Hanoi only a couple days—"

"Yes, yes, I have been following you, now keep your voice down. I will tell you who I am."

I did as she said and sat back in my chair queasily.

She cleared her throat and leaned farther over the table. Her movements were fluid, self-assured. She kept her eyes trained on mine with unwavering intensity. "I am an operative with Abeeku Boateng's private security force."

"You're one of his bodyguards?"

"No, not like that. We are a group hired covertly by Mr. Boateng to conduct espionage in the service of Ghanaian independence, amongst other duties."

"Then I would have to assume you know he's dead, right?"

"Yes, of course, and please lower your voice. Of course we know he is dead, that is why I am here. I take it that you, on the other hand, are somewhat confused."

My instinct was to deflate into a vulnerable mess when she said this. I wanted to believe she could provide me with any answers at all, but I was wary of her and managed to keep my face blank.

"We have been trying to track you down and confirm your identity for weeks. After Mr. Boateng was assassinated, the operatives who infiltrated Kente wiped the files of the computers and surveillance systems, and murdered his guards."

"Assassinated? But he was killed by the ceiling fan in his office."

"Yes, we know. It was all planned, including you being there when it happened."

A molten rush of adrenaline. Back at the hotel in Ghana I had suspected my having witnessed Boateng's death wasn't a coincidence, but the more time that had passed without any clear indications of what was going on led my thinking to become distorted, wishful even, and I had started to secretly hope my involvement was nothing more than a mistake.

"Me? But what do I have to do with any of this? Who are you that you know this?"

"Calm down. I told you, I am part of Mr. Boateng's private security force. It is not unusual. Many powerful CEOs and corporations employ private security teams."

"What?"

She looked at me like she would a pitiable, ignorant creature. "The World Org is not so stable as you might imagine. The oligarchs who control the major conglomerates have slowly gained more power in the government bureaucracy, to the point where they are now almost on an equal footing with the politicians.

Because of this, the government is becoming less effective at restraining infighting between the largest financial forces. They are becoming bolder, acting like regional powers. They employ their own small private armies. I do not doubt Mr. Boateng made clear to you his nationalist views during your meeting with him?"

"Yes," I said. "More than clear."

She nodded, dropping her gaze from mine for the first time since she'd sat down. She spoke with bitter regret. "He was a brilliant man, but he had no talent for subtlety. We warned him it was his words that would get him in trouble rather than his actions. We could not control him because he cared for Ghana passionately, and for that I considered him a true leader, but now we see what passion without calculation has gotten us."

"So they killed him because he was a nationalist. What does that have to do with me?"

"He was not just a nationalist. Up until a few weeks ago he was essentially the ruler of the African Zone. He expanded Kente into the economic engine of the continent and suppressed his competitors, with our help, through shadow conflict. Our conviction, which Mr. Boateng shared, is that the W.O. has only continued the trend of overlooking and exploiting Africa, just like all the great powers that came before it. Mr. Boateng had a vision of a united, independent continent, with Ghana acting as its leader. He was destabilizing the system of oligarchy and leadership in the zone, and because of his lack of caution he became a target worthy of elimination."

"You're a nationalist, too."

"Yes. But we have had to go into hiding since Abeeku's death. They are hunting us down."

"Who?"

"Basil & Crittenden. Alaafia. An alliance of other, smaller oligarchs, all undoubtedly acting in concert with the World Org."

"B&C? But why would they be involved in this?"

"As it turns out, because of you."

I was at a loss.

"They are engineering you as a scapegoat for his death."

"*What?* I don't— I don't understand, why me?"

"Quiet. I am able to cloak us from face-rec cameras and localized mics, but it won't mean anything if they pick up ambient audio."

I leaned forward in my chair, not caring anymore who heard what. "*Tell* me."

She appeared irritated at my refusal to keep my voice down, but she answered anyway. "Because you represented the opportunity for a perfect fall-man. You are a convicted felon of lower treason due to your mother's activities as a former anti-W.O. ultra-nationalist, and you are classified with an unstable mental disorder. With these two things they can cast an image of you as a murderous ideologue."

"But if I'm supposed to be an ultra-nationalist, why would I kill Boateng?"

"They intend to connect you to *us*. In order to be able to track down and eliminate the remaining networks of African nationalists in full view of the public, they will conceal Mr. Boateng's beliefs, and indeed that he was the one who established our nationalist network in the first place. They will depict us as an independently-operating, anti-W.O. terrorist group that wanted the CEO of Kente, Inc. dead because he was attempting to put a stop to our activities in Ghana. We would have used you as a mole inside Basil & Crittenden to gain personal access to him, and you killed Mr. Boateng. That will be the official version."

I was holding my breath, feeling suddenly surrounded. People continued to walk past the patio, to sit down at the tables.

"How do you know all this?"

"We had an operative inside Machie Obode's inner circle. One of our Nigerian brothers. He managed to get us this information, but we have not heard from him since."

Thoughts rocketed through my head. "If they're going to pin his death on me, then why haven't they done it yet? There hasn't been anything in the news. No one knows anything and they've let me go anywhere I wanted to."

"That is not entirely true. They summoned you back to New Boston so you could be diagnosed as entering an advanced phase of your mental disorder. They would not have been able to do it before you left to Ghana, otherwise you would have had to be sent to a psych facility."

I thought about my evaluation with Roorback. The aggressiveness of his interrogation, his avoidance of my questions, finally his quick decision to update the status of my BPD to a premorbid phase and to approve my work clearance. But how could they have known I would be in the hospital and subject to a mandatory psych eval? Unless they *deliberately* gave me food poisoning in order to evaluate and then reassign me. A shiver uncoiled itself within my chest.

"I still don't understand, why haven't they pinned the murder on me yet? Why are they waiting?"

"We do not understand that either. In any case, it does not matter. You, me, all my nationalist brothers and sisters, we are all as good as dead. All we can do is hope to outwit the World Org agents about to close in."

"Then why come looking for me?"

Her eyes narrowed in something like accusation. "You have an enormous amount of money in your possession."

I broke into a stutter, hoping to defend myself.

"I do not need explanations, and I don't care. But I will tell you this. What is absolutely certain is that they are watching you, and without our help you will be captured. You don't seem so oblivious as to think you are outrunning them."

"No."

"Then you know you have no other option except to come with me. The chances are slim, but we may be able to survive if we go deep into hiding. Our capabilities are enough to do this, but we must have the unmarked scrips. Right now, I am your only friend."

She was right. Or at least she was the only friend I knew of. Although I wasn't able to implicitly trust her, what she was saying sounded true. Worst was that the small optimism she was offering, minimal as it was and ridiculous as I felt, resurrected a blind hope inside me that maybe I could still get out of all this. I had to go with her, for better or worse.

I took her to my hotel where we transferred the scrips into a bag she told me was cloaked with a false identity inside the object network. She gave me a counterfeit ID and adhered a tiny transmitter under my arm that would cause any face-rec cameras to confuse me as someone else. We headed straight to the airport where we purchased tickets for a flight to Ghana. Security didn't stop us. Emma, throughout everything, was silent except for when she needed to communicate with me. If I tried to talk to her she replied only with curt, closed-off responses. After a while I couldn't tell if she was stoic or traumatized. I only wished she was a more comforting travel companion. My brain overworked itself with everything she had told me during the brutally long flight. I didn't sleep. I played and replayed my entire life, coming to ever more frightening conclusions that perhaps everything that had ever happened to me was part of one big overarching conspiracy, that nothing I'd ever done had really been my own decision, that—

I rushed to the bathroom and puked into the sink. Something was wrong with me, and it wasn't just the shock of the situation. Something about my body, my consciousness, felt immaterial. I felt the full crushing weight of things, and yet it seemed, in an impossible to define way, that I was outside of myself, simply watching as events unfolded.

Touching down back in New Accra for a second time brought with it a fresh sense of phantasmagoria. I felt as if a dozen lifetimes had passed.

Finally, Emma provided me with the barest words of encouragement.

"It is going to be all right," she said as we walked out of the airport to meet our ride.

I nodded. "I hope so."

An unassuming four-door economy car pulled up to the curb. "In the back," she said.

I opened the door and got in. There was a man with a bald head and sunglasses sitting next to me, Emma and the driver up front.

"Drive," she said.

The traffic was not heavy, and we quickly sped onto the same freeway that I had taken with Boateng to go tour the city not even a month ago. No one spoke. I looked out the window at the skyline rising up clear and precise this time against a hot African sun.

"Stanly," Emma said in the front seat.

"Yeah?"

I looked at the man to my left and saw he was now pointing a handgun at me. The car was hushed. In his other hand he was holding out a piece of black cloth. The lenses of his sunglasses gaped at me remorseless, perched above an ironclad mouth.

It was Emma's voice that commanded me from the front, but she did not turn around. "Put on the hood, Stanly. I'm sorry to have done this to you, but we have no choice."

I sighed, still feeling oddly untethered to my own body. I took the hood and pulled it down over my head. This time I did take the opportunity to sleep.

I was taken out of the car with someone's hand around my neck and the snout of the pistol shoved against my spine. By the heavy odor of spices alone I could tell I was back somewhere in or around Dansoman market. My ears fizzled with the background noise of constant, glimmering voices. They marched me forward. A door closed and I was shoved down into a chair, my hands pulled behind my back and tied together exceedingly tight. The hood was pulled off my head.

We were inside a single-room concrete house with a roof made of corrugated steel. Aside from a few large storage chests sitting against the walls, the room was bare. A sooty layer of shadow coated the room. Just enough natural light shined in through the windows, covered by tapestries, that Emma and the two other men were visible. The man with the bald head threw the hood to the floor and took off his sunglasses, revealing high-strung, yellowish eyes.

"Keep your mouth shut," he told me.

Emma stood with the driver, a spindly man with long, excitable limbs and braids pulled back into a ponytail.

"I still say keeping him with us is a foolish idea," he said to Emma.

She responded calm as ever. "You have to trust, Coba. There are hardly any pieces on the board in this game, and our best bet is to control as many as possible."

He wore a metallic-blue suit that hugged tight to his slender frame. "But we are not controlling anything. They know what we are up to. They must know we have him."

"They might, but they do not know where we are. I followed him for days and did not see any operatives. They always rely too much on the surveillance network."

"*Bah.* You are too confident." He walked up to me and looked me over, long hands on narrow hips. His lips puffed out to where his thin mustache was up against his nostrils, brow scrunched down in thought. "I say we kill him."

The bald man stood off to one side with his hands held together militarily in front of him. He cast a look in Emma's direction.

"That would be the stupidest thing we could do," she said, turning to him and exuding an air of offended authority. "They have no reason to keep us alive except for the fear we might harm him. Take that away and we have nothing."

"We should kill him," Coba persisted. "They expect us to use him as leverage to save ourselves. If he is already dead they will have to change their plans. That would give us time to take the money and disappear."

All three were silent for a moment. An extreme tension hung between Emma and the spindly man, as if he were rebelling against her.

Coba extended a pole-like arm toward the bald man with yellowish eyes. "Nkrumah. What do you think?"

Nkrumah folded his arms, taking a second to deliberate. "I agree with Emma," he said finally. "What do we gain by killing him?"

"What do we gain by not?" Coba shot back. "If we have him here, it is only because they allowed it."

"You don't know that, Coba," Emma coolly rejoined.

"But how could it be otherwise? We are both of us only assuming the way things are, but at least my plan disrupts theirs."

My eyes focused in on a waterfall of dust motes surging through a gold bar of sunlight slanting across my knees. My hands throbbed painfully behind me with my heartbeat, and I thought that, to die here, in this moment, it was not enough, that maybe no place or moment in time could be enough.

"We are responsible for the lives of many people," Nkrumah said. "I say we err on the side of caution."

"Think about it," Coba said, this time appealing to Emma, as if she'd been the one who might listen to him all along. "Keeping him with us keeps a target on our backs. He is important to them, that is why we tried to get to him first, but they need him more than we do. All we need is the money. If we kill him, everything they have tried to orchestrate turns out to be for nothing, and we go into hiding. Nothing changes except for the fact that they miscalculated by letting him fall into our hands. We know they intend to connect his supposed motivations for killing Abeeku to us. Why would they not want us to capture him?"

Emma looked at the floor, considering what Coba was saying more carefully this time. Nkrumah stood with his arms still folded, fidgeting in the expanse of silence and looking first at Emma, then at Coba. Apparently he could no longer stand it. "We discussed this before. We agreed he was valuable as leverage. What has changed between now and then?"

Coba turned to give me another ponderous overview. "Nothing

has changed. It is just an idea."

The heat inside the house had become uncomfortable. All three of their faces were filmed over with sweat. The tip of my own nose dripped steadily. Emma spoke up from her position in the darkest part of the room, her face made almost completely opaque by a drape of hot shadow.

"Coba is not necessarily wrong."

"But what about the unity of Ghana?" Nkrumah said, incredulous of what he was hearing. "How do we continue fighting for our nation if all that is left for us to do is go into hiding?"

Coba leaned against one of the storage chests, dejected, letting out a groan of stress. "How can we work for unity if we are dead?"

"All that is over, anyway, Nkrumah," Emma said. "Without Abeeku, there is no Ghanaian unity. He was the key, the only thing keeping our operation safe. This has become a matter of survival."

"I refuse to believe that. The nationalist networks we built are still out there, still operational, and we have the upper hand. If we are able to avoid being captured or killed, what is stopping us from continuing the work?"

Coba flew back into a standing position, nearly shouting. "Upper hand?"

"Yes, we have him as our hostage, we —"

"You have not spent nearly as much time as we have building those nationalist networks you speak of," Emma scolded, trying to reassert her control over the two of them. "I worked for Abeeku for sixteen years in pursuit of an independent Ghana. If I say there is no unity without him, it is not because I am giving up, it is because I know what I am talking about. There is a reason they assassinated him. What we are talking about here is the safety of the group."

Coba seemed to be growing more agitated, pacing around and touching his face like the full seriousness of everything was descending on him all at once. His thin legs swayed like a huge bird.

"*Now*," she commanded, "I'm starting to think Coba may have a good point."

"We should just kill him now," Coba said, impatience rising into his voice. "We're running out of time. They won't wait much longer now that we have brought him here."

"Settle down. There is time to think this through."

"For the record," Nkrumah said, "I am not in agreement with killing him."

"You are both going to get us killed if we wait much longer!"

"Coba, I am ordering you to calm down!"

I interrupted them. "He's right," I said.

The three of them stopped their conversation and looked at me.

I repeated myself. "He's right. Coba is right. If they're planning to implicate me with your organization, they most likely wanted you to take me hostage." My words came out in painful spurts as I tried to ignore the exploding pain in my hands. "Kill me and make a run for it. It's the only thing they won't expect."

They stood stunned. I believed what I had said. Coba's idea was the only one that made sense, but Emma seemed reluctant to do it out of principle. I *wanted* them to escape. Giving them permission to kill me was the only way I could change the outcome of their struggle for the better, a struggle that reminded me of my mother's. And it was the only way to ruin the plans the W.O., or corporate cabal, or whoever, had for me after this was all over. I wanted to make a difference, for myself and them.

After a moment, Nkrumah blurted out dismissively, "He is suicidal! Or maybe he wants to see us killed now that we kidnapped him." He held out his arms in my direction, pleading them to perceive my insanity.

"No," I said evenly. "I'm not suicidal. I'm in this as much as you, but I have no chance of getting away. You do. If you kill me, you take away their scapegoat for Boateng's murder. Please. You would be doing me a favor."

Again, the silence seemed to say that what I was proposing made sense.

"We cannot trust him," Nkrumah said.

Emma placed a contemplative hand against her mouth, thinking. Coba looked at them both, looked at me, his alarm growing at an intolerable rate the longer Emma stayed quiet.

Nkrumah entreated Emma again, more desperate this time. "He is suicidal, we should stick to the plan!"

She seemed stuck, unable to come to a decision.

Coba broke, pulling a chrome gun from a holster inside his jacket and leveling it straight at me. "If you cannot decide, Emma, I am going to decide for you!"

Emma thundered. "Coba! Stop!"

I squeezed my eyes shut and took a gasping breath.

Multiple gunshots reverberated like bomb blasts in the concrete structure. I felt no pain and opened my eyes to see Coba spilling dead onto the floor, Nkrumah's gun drawn and the muzzle flashing two, three times more.

Emma ran behind the storage chest against the wall next to her, drawing her gun and firing at Nkrumah.

"You fucking dog! I knew it!" The sound of her curses were perforated by her own pistol shots.

He dove at my chair and toppled me over sideways. The left side of my face smacked the floor, but still I spotted Emma rising from behind her cover with her weapon aimed at me, meaning to finish what Nkrumah had tried to stop them from doing. She fired and I felt a shattering pain detonate through the middle of my arm. She was unable to get another shot before Nkrumah layed down a wild volley of defensive fire. The darkened room flickered with the light from his gun. The front door suddenly burst open with a crash. Emma spun to defend herself, but before she could there came the fluttering report of an assault rifle. She was only able to let out a horrid half-scream before there was no sound left save for the ringing in my ears.

Several armored tactical soldiers entered through the rectangle of blazing light, surveying the bloody scene.

I heard Nkrumah's voice behind me. "Fuck! You should have been here two minutes ago! They almost killed him!"

For the first time, I had wanted to make a difference. Change things for the better. The way it turned out was, nothing could be changed, and no difference could've been made. The nationalists had been infiltrated, and any hope of going into hiding, for both them and me, had been false. As for the W.O., everything had gone according to plan. If only they had killed me.

I was immediately taken to a hospital by the tac squad to have my gunshot wound treated. High Org agents stood guard outside my room in ICU. The bullet hadn't caused much damage to my arm. I was told by one of the agents that I would be moved into police custody the next day.

I couldn't get rid of the agonizing sense of being humiliated. I had given up a long time ago, accepted my fate as incontrovertible, so why should I feel like this? I remembered the flight back to Ghana with Emma, throwing up in the sink. I had felt so powerless, so inconsequential to the events of my own life it had been like my body was spontaneously disassembling, my thoughts and soul vaporizing into a gaseous nothingness. Somehow, in imploring them to kill me, I had zapped back into existence. For a brief instant, I believed I could change things. In retrospect, lying in the stillness of the hospital room, the moment seemed seminal, radiant even, and then, within the context of my current situation, it transformed into a vision of horror—that small glowing ember of something, of *hope*, had appeared to me, and quickly floated beyond my grasp.

One of the guards came into the room. He looked around as if searching for something before his gaze landed on me. He regarded my incapacitated figure in the bed with total disinterest. He turned, reached toward the screen that hung from the ceiling in front of me, clicked it on and cycled through several channels before finding the one he was looking for. He turned up the volume and left the room.

It was the news. The story I'd been waiting to see ever since Boateng's death had now, of course, magically surfaced.

KENTE, INC. CEO MURDERED

Ultra-nationalist assassin had ties to
Ghanaian independence terror cell

Veronika Petrova interviewing a martial-looking woman whose name and title was listed as *Nina Ulrich, High Org Department of Investigations.*

"And, Nina, please, can you describe this individual? Who is he, and do you know his reasons for doing this?"

"Yes, we know his reasons. The individual's name is Stanly Borque. We know he was employed very recently with Basil & Crittenden in their marketing department, and that he's the son of Elizabeth Borque, who was one of the founders of the ultra-nationalist group IFA that had as its stated objective the overthrow of the World Organization government. Evaluators had determined him to be unstable, I'm told he was very recently classified by the DMHE as having a 'morbid phase borderline personality.' What we know at this time is that Mr. Borque acted in a covert capacity for an ultra-nationalist terrorist group in Ghana, who targeted

Mr. Boateng in an effort to spread fear and chaos within that internation and the African Zone more generally. Mr. Borque has quite an incriminating past, he was previously convicted of lower treason in the wake of his mother's illegal activities, along with—"

Over her voice, images of myself. A slow zoom-in on the smiling portrait I took for my B&C entry badge. Looping footage of me rushing out of the lobby of the Kente offices after Boateng had died, appearing disheveled and paranoid. Footage of Emma and I at the cafe in New Sydney, and then of us walking together through the airport. Grainy thumbnail photos of her and Coba. I still didn't understand. All this video evidence could have been easily digitally engineered, so why go to the trouble of orchestrating something so elaborate? They didn't need to do all that just to deceive the public. Obviously something else was at work.

If only they had killed me.

The next day they transferred me to police headquarters. Leaving the hospital, one of the High Org agents held a jacket over my head to keep me hidden from the press, who had congregated outside in massive numbers. This was part of the final act of the show. The ultra-nationalist terrorist in captivity. My show trial and sentencing would serve as the catharsis.

Once into police custody they provided me a meal and had another doctor examine me. Afterwards I was taken to an interrogation room and told to wait. The room was a bleached, fluorescent-lit cube, fully bereft of shadow, the walls seeming to breathe with the humming quality of the bulbs. A lightweight metal desk and chairs. A two-way mirror in one wall. I sat down and waited, unsure whether I should tell the truth, or simply tell them what they wanted to hear to get the whole thing over with quicker.

Twenty minutes felt like a very long time just sitting in the interrogation room. I had the sense they were making me wait longer than they should. I fidgeted in the hard chair to stay comfortable. Eventually I knew at least half an hour had gone by, probably more. I got up and walked to the two-way mirror, wondering what was going on. They were most likely doing it on purpose, and even if I complained they wouldn't care. I found myself walking in endless circles around the desk. Time kept passing, and for some reason I tried to keep a handle on it, but once I was fairly certain two hours had passed I was no longer able to know what the span of an hour felt like. I went around and around in the shadowless room. My feet started to hurt, and I sat down on the chair, but it wasn't comfortable so I laid on the floor.

Time turned to sheer banality. Table, chairs, walls, ceiling, floor, mirror, chairs, ceiling, chairs. An endless reduction of the room and an endless, abhorrent expansion of myself. My thoughts themselves seemed to be broadcast to me from a booming speaker somewhere in the walls. At first I was self-conscious at the idea of someone watching me through the mirror, but I stopped caring and got to know the corners of the floor, every nuance of the chairs. I inspected the polished grain of the desk's brushed metal finish, running the pads of my fingers across its texture. I assumed more than half a day had passed.

The door opened and I scrambled to my feet. A man in a grey suit came in holding a water pitcher and glass. He was well-fed but thin, his neck a bit out of proportion with his head.

"Hello, Stanly. We're sorry about the wait, but I brought you something to drink."

"I need to use the bathroom."

"Sure, sure," he said, walking past me to set the water on the desk like I'd only been waiting in there a few minutes. "Just hang tight for a little longer, we'll take you to the bathroom."

"Please," I said.

"A little longer, just hold on." He disappeared through the door.

I gravitated to the pitcher and poured myself a glass of water. My throat had turned to sand. The liquid washed over my mouth clear, cold, delicious. Breathing some relief, I sat down in one of the chairs for the first time in a long time, hoping to show whoever was watching me that I was ready and willing to cooperate. Suddenly I could feel the minutes again. Ten, fifteen. I leaned against the desk, both somehow yawning and brooding at an uncontrollable pace.

I started to feel something. I wasn't sure what, but it came as a surprise, my body slowly ensconced by a tingling euphoria and my vision becoming hypersensitive, infinitely recursive, feeding my thoughts and my thoughts feeding my vision, a swirling, pulsing soup of alphanumerics, images, sensations. Something in the water.

Time gelled. Man came in the room. Same man. Sat down in chair.

"—kay, Stanly, what I'd like you to do is to answer some questions for us, can you do—"

Man has job, wakes up in morning, takes shower, eats something. Has job, greets coworkers good morning, thinks of coworkers as friends. Wears underwear, washes hands. Has thoughts but thoughts aren't correct. Gets up in morning, acts as instrument. Man is two people at same time. I am, too.

"—want to know if you can tell us why you decided to murder Mr. Boateng—"

Lungs work, brain works, hands move. Go to job, go to sleep. Sleep feels good. Food tastes good. Do things you do to feel good. Go to job, do things they tell you. Man wakes up, man drinks coffee, man puts on clothes he doesn't wear at home, man knows certain things, knows how to think, how to act. Gets a haircut, shaves. Job is just a job, just a job. Things are the way things are. Why do things. Why act. There is life for man, but is there reason to live. Does man, talking to me in a room, have the right to demand that reality make sense.

"—long have you been affiliated with the Ghanaian terror cell?"

Swallow. Who makes sense.

"Stanly?"

Time to speak up. Which words will come out.

Unsteady, but certain. "If I can't make my own destiny, what am I? A piece of errata. No will. No influence. It means I don't exist. Just inert, like some kind of device. Some kind of recording device."

Man is quiet. Just doing his job.

"You're going to prison for a long time."

ABOUT THE AUTHOR

Steven T. Bramble was born in 1986 in Pueblo, CO. He is the author of the Psychology of Technology trilogy (*Affliction Included*, *Grid City Overload*, *Disposable Thought*), a thematically-connected series of novels that questions the implications of modernity. He is a co-founder of ZQ-287 Press and lives in Long Beach.